FOUR SOLDIERS

Also by Hubert Mingarelli

A Meal in Winter

Four Soldiers

Hubert Mingarelli

*Translated from the French
by Sam Taylor*

Portobello
Books

Published by Portobello Books 2018

Portobello Books
12 Addison Avenue
London
W11 4QR

Copyright © Hubert Mingarelli 2003
English translation © Sam Taylor 2018

Originally published in French as *Quatre Soldats*
by Éditions de Seuil in 2003

A CIP catalogue record is available from the British Library

9 8 7 6 5 4 3 2 1

ISBN 978 1 84627 650 7
eISBN 978 1 84627 652 1

www.portobellobooks.com

Typeset in Bembo by Patty Rennie

Printed and bound by CPI Group (UK) Ltd,
Croydon, CR0 4YY

I

I AM FROM Dorovitsa in the province of Vyatka. When my parents died I left Dorovitsa and moved to Kalyazin, by the river, where I worked for a man named Ovanes.

I harnessed felled tree trunks to a horse to transport them from the riverbank to the sawmill. Then I tied them to a winch and lowered them one by one to Ovanes' band saw. In the evening I fed the horse with oats and spread out straw for him.

I rented a room from Ovanes at 16 Svevo Street. My window overlooked the river. I had a bed and a rug. I built myself a cabinet where I kept my belongings.

I was alone in the world and in the evening I watched the river as I ate. There were flat-bottomed boats moving upstream. Their hulls gleamed in the setting sun. On the bridge the shadows were like ghosts.

When I left Kalyazin, Ovanes bought the bed, the rug and the cabinet from me. I took the train to join the Red Army and I fought on the Romanian front. We marched a long way. We ate cold kasha and dried fish and we slept in ditches.

I was in Dudorov's regiment, and in the summer we fled from the Romanians. It was very hot. The cavalry kicked up clouds of red dust. The ambulance and food-truck drivers yelled at us to get out of the way. The officers stopped to look behind them, hands shielding their eyes from the sun, as if they'd forgotten something.

Then I met Pavel. He was heating up some water behind a wall, hidden from the road. He'd stabbed a hole in a tin can with his knife and he was holding it above the flames. Our regiment continued to march along the road, kicking up dust.

When he took some tea out of his pocket, my thirst and the sight of the tea emboldened me. I called out to him: 'Hey, comrade!'

He beckoned me over. I sat across from him and we drank the tea together in silence. We were in the same regiment. When the noise from the road had died down completely, I said to him: 'The Romanians will be here soon.'

We set off, and caught up with the tail end of the column. An officer on horseback was circling around the tired soldiers, trying to hurry them up. He'd put a handkerchief under his cap to protect the back of his neck from the sun.

He was red from the dust and he held his revolver against his stomach. He kept saying, over and over: 'I know you're tired, but don't make me do it. I swear by Saint Sophia, don't make me. Keep going! Don't slow down!'

And as he said this he moved the revolver from his stomach and held it in his fingertips as if it were burning hot. He was a young sub-lieutenant and he looked on the verge of tears. Finally, a soldier who was pulling a mule by its bridle said to him: 'What do you want from us? We're marching, we're marching. Put your revolver away. No one's making you do anything.'

The officer yelled: 'What did you say to me?'

The soldier lowered his head. The officer went up to him, brandishing his revolver. He put the barrel of the gun to the mule's neck and pulled the trigger. It fell forwards. The soldier had wrapped the bridle around his wrist and he fell onto the road too, dragged down by the mule and its load.

The officer stood above them, his revolver pointed at the sky. In a rage, he screamed: 'No one's making me do anything, eh? You feel better now?'

The soldier was lying on his back, covered in the mule's blood. He stared darkly at the officer and said in a cold voice: 'Bastard.'

3

The soldier tried to grab his rifle but it was trapped under his back. He pushed the mule away to free himself and picked up his knife. So Pavel and I both ran towards the ditch, hurtling down into it and coming out the other side, and then into a field to get away from the road.

It was a sloping field, the grass cut short.

When we reached the high part of the field, we could see the column stretched out all the way to the horizon. This was exactly what we wanted: not to lose sight of the others, to keep marching eastward with them to escape the Romanians, but without having to deal with all the troubles on the road.

We paused to get our breath back.

It felt suddenly hot and I took out my tobacco.

We heard a bird singing from behind a hedge.

We spat out the remains of the dust from our throats. In the distance they were turning on the headlights of the ambulances and trucks.

We looked all around us.

Then we set off again, smoking our cigarettes in the evening light, and I imagined we were returning from a hunting expedition. Pavel looked peaceful as he walked. He could sense which way to go even in the darkness. Sometimes he would sniff the air. After a while he said to me:

'We'll join them on the road tomorrow. No one will notice we were ever gone.'

'You're right,' I said, 'no one will notice.'

It was a clear night except for one dark strip of cloud on the horizon and we spread out our blankets under some mulberry trees.

At dawn we rejoined the regiment, and as we were approaching the road Pavel said: 'Let's stay together.'

'Yeah.'

We continued our retreat from the Romanians and in September we travelled to Galicia in trucks.

One night in Galicia, Pavel took a table and two chairs out of a house and we played dice in the middle of the street. A big Uzbek from our company stood at a distance and watched us play. He had broad shoulders. He was built like a lumberjack and sometimes he seemed a bit slow.

Pavel told him to come over. He asked him if he had any tobacco. The Uzbek did, and he wanted to gamble it at dice. He went to fetch another chair from the house and we played a dozen games. Pavel won all his tobacco and the Uzbek stayed sitting at the table, looking miserable. Pavel watched him with a smile, and in the end he gave him back half of his tobacco. The Uzbek was very grateful. He looked so happy now that you'd have thought he was the one who'd won every game.

When we went back into the house to sleep, the Uzbek went off to find his belongings and his rifle. He moved in with us and we didn't object. The next day he lit a fire and we made a soup with his rations. While Pavel and I ate, still wrapped up in our blankets, and the daylight came in through the window, the big Uzbek stared at us with his blank idiot's expression and we realised that he wanted more than anything to stay with us. When Pavel asked him his name, he blushed and suddenly he didn't look like an idiot any more. 'Kyabine!' he boomed.

That day, the Poles took the village back from us. They ambushed us near Jarosław and things started going badly for us again.

In October it snowed and we waited in a factory for our orders. When they arrived, our commander brought us together and told us that we had to leave the front and retreat into the forest. There, we would build huts and wait for the spring. So Pavel, Kyabine and I wandered all over the factory, looking for anything that might be useful in the forest, and we found a rolled-up tarpaulin.

We left the next day. Kyabine carried the heavy tarp roll over his shoulder. On the way we saw the Poles again. More than once we had to run to avoid being caught by gunfire, and Kyabine never once let go of the tarpaulin.

We reached the forest in early November and marched deep inside it. It was very cold and the wind blew relentlessly. We wrapped ourselves up in our blankets, covering everything but our eyes. The whole company advanced in a vast silence. Our mules and our horses breathed out clouds of steam.

Pavel walked at the back of the column and said nothing because in his head he was drawing up the plans for our hut.

It started to snow again. Kyabine walked heavily next to me. He breathed with his mouth open. Sometimes he shook himself to knock the snow from his shoulders.

Pavel caught up with us and he told us that he had the hut clear in his mind now. And the best thing, he thought, would be to have four of us to build it. We told him he was right. We had a discussion to decide who we would ask to join us. We gave our opinions on lots of men in the company. Finally we went to ask Sifra Nedatchin. He was very young and a good shot, and he owned cavalry boots. We'd never heard of him having any trouble with anyone about anything.

He was walking on his own behind a mule and when he saw us approaching he was frightened. It was Pavel who asked him if he'd like to help us build a hut and live in it with us. He said yes in a shy voice. I handed out cigarettes to everyone.

The company marched for three days in the falling snow, the bitter cold and the fierce wind. Then we cut down some trees to form a clearing.

We all began building huts. About thirty of them went up in the snow, forming a circle around the edge of the clearing.

We built ours following Pavel's plans. Kyabine showed how strong he was. He got through more work than Pavel, Sifra and me combined. While the three of us paused to catch our breath, Kyabine valiantly kept going.

When we'd finished building our hut, we proudly contemplated it in the light of the fire that burned at the centre of the clearing. We walked all around it, congratulating one another, and then all four of us went inside and I thought to myself: That's it, I'm not alone in the world any more. And I was right.

2

WE WERE OUT of the forest now. Winter was over and it is difficult to imagine how long and cold it had been. We had eaten our mules and our horses, and many of our men had died in the forest. Some of them died when their huts caught fire. Or they got lost when they were out hunting. Soldiers who went hunting later found their bodies. Of course some of the ones we didn't find must have deserted. But I think in most cases they just got lost and froze to death.

The four of us were still alive and kicking, thanks to Pavel. He was the cleverest of us all. His plans for the hut were perfect, and he was even able to build a real stove using a metal barrel filled with engine oil. A real stove that worked well and didn't smoke us out. But most importantly he'd found a way to pass the pipe through the roof without setting fire to it. Because that was how most of the other huts caught fire. Pavel had made tin tiles by cutting up our mess tins and then he'd nailed them to the roof around the pipe. So we'd had to sacrifice half of our mess tins and steal a few from the company in order to make those tiles. But we were still alive. And not once did we wake in the night, terrified and covered in sweat, dreaming that our hut was going up in smoke.

As for the tarpaulin that Kyabine had carried from Galicia to the forest, we used it to keep out draughts.

There was no peat in the forest. We had to shift large quantities of snow every day to uncover dead trees for fuel. The men who'd chosen to cut down the trees that grew nearby ended up with green wood, and they were a lot less warm than we were.

All winter long, we shifted snow and collected wood for our stove, and in the evenings we were able to play dice because we had a lamp and oil. Thanks to that lamp, we suffered far less from boredom than others in the company.

When the spring arrived, the company set fire to all the huts. Pavel, Kyabine, Sifra and I were sad as we watched ours burn. Not because we were leaving, but because that hut had kept us warm and alive through all those months.

As we walked away from the fire, I spoke in my head to my parents: Look at me, you don't have to be afraid for me any more because I survived the winter and I have comrades now.

And we left the forest.

3

WE WERE OUT in the plain, sitting on a pile of old railway sleepers. The tracks were just in front of us. An armoured train had just passed. Some of the soldiers, standing on the running board, waved to us, their shirts flapping under their arms.

The camp was not far away. We'd built it at the edge of a pine wood. Our company's commander was a shy man who left us to our own devices. We didn't know what he used to do, before the war. I'm sure he always wished that the soldiers who'd got lost in the forest, and who we imagined frozen to death, had in reality deserted.

We were on that pile of sleepers, doing nothing. We were just happy that the winter was over and that we'd found this place to sit, and we were peacefully smoking our cigarettes. From time to time a flock of birds flew across the sky. We looked up and watched them disappear northwards. Soon they would be flying over the forest where we'd spent the winter. We probably all thought this, but none of us said anything.

As usual, Kyabine asked us for tobacco because he almost always lost his at dice, and had done ever since the first games in Galicia. It was Sifra who gave him the most. Pavel and I gave him some too, but not so often, and we liked to wait until he begged us for it. Kyabine was like a child when he asked us for tobacco. He was like a child in lots of other ways too, but when it came to tobacco he really was one.

'Pavel!' said Kyabine.

'What do you want?' Pavel asked him.

'Roll me a cigarette.'

Pavel continued to stare straight ahead.

Kyabine insisted: 'Pavel? Oh, Pavel!'

'What, Kyabine?'

'Didn't you hear me? Please give me some tobacco.'

As I said, Pavel and I liked it when Kyabine started begging.

4

WE CLIMBED DOWN from the sleepers, picked up our rifles and set off across the fields. Kyabine was walking in front of me. He'd finally got a bit of tobacco from Pavel, and even from behind I could tell he was very happy that he could smoke.

We went to the pond.

Soon after that we heard Yassov, calling from behind. He too found it hard to make his way through the tall grass. He caught up and walked alongside us. We didn't pay any attention to him because we already knew what he wanted. He reached into his pocket and took out a hand sculpted in wood, then showed it to us. We laughed because it was very big.

'Why are you laughing?' Yassov asked.

Pavel said: 'It's not your big fat hand we want, Yassov, it's a fiancée's hand.'

'I can make it a bit smaller if you want.'

'Bugger off, Yassov!' said Pavel. 'And take your hand with you.'

'Yeah, bugger off,' echoed Kyabine.

Yassov continued to walk alongside us. He wasn't giving up. He stared seriously at the sculpted hand, turning it over, then said: 'Listen, I think I can make it quite a bit smaller. You're right.'

Kyabine started grunting in Yassov's face, making strange sounds like a steam engine. Pavel, Sifra and I imitated him, and suddenly it was as if we were in a steam-engine factory.

So Yassov gave up trying to sell us the hand for tobacco. He stopped walking, and behind us we heard him shout: 'Bloody idiots!'

His voice echoed in the air above the field and we continued advancing through the tall grass. Again, but more quietly, we heard him shout: 'Bloody idiots!'

Yassov had started sculpting these women's hands when we were in the forest. He'd sold several in return for food rations. With those hands, the men who didn't have a fiancée were perhaps able to imagine that they did. As for the men who did have fiancées, well, perhaps it helped them to remember them.

Now we weren't so short of food, it was tobacco that he asked for in return.

To start with, the hands he sculpted were quite pretty. But they were so delicate that, when the men slept with them, they broke, and then the men yelled at Yassov. That was why Yassov was sculpting more solid hands now. But the problem was they looked like men's hands. Even Kyabine's hands weren't as big as those wooden hands. No one could possibly have wanted a fiancée with hands like that.

We continued walking and we smelled the pond before we saw it.

We had been very lucky to discover this pond. We'd already spent a lot of time there since coming out of the forest. For the moment, we were the only ones who went there. But we lived in constant fear that other men from the company would discover it. If that happened we'd probably have to fight them, because we had no intention of sharing our pond.

Kyabine and Pavel waded into the water up to their knees. Sifra and I stayed on the bank. We didn't like swimming. Sifra lay on his back and looked up at the sky. I watched Pavel and Kyabine as they went in up to their waists. Around them the water had grown muddy. Kyabine tried to make the water clear again by stirring it with his hands. Pavel moved away from him. He crouched down and now all I saw was his head sticking out of the water.

Pavel and Kyabine went swimming while Sifra fell asleep next to me. This was a precious place. Because we didn't know where we would be tomorrow. We had come out of the forest, the winter was over, but we didn't know how much time we would stay here, nor where we would have to go next. The war wasn't over, but as usual we didn't know anything about the army's operations. It was better not to think about it. We could already count ourselves lucky to have found this pond.

When Pavel and Kyabine returned to the bank they were covered in mud. They sat down and waited for the sun to dry them before they got dressed again.

We would have liked to shoot our rifles at the water, but as we wanted to keep the pond a secret we knew it was best not to make too much noise. That would have attracted the attention of the rest of the company.

Pavel and Kyabine stood up and rubbed themselves. The mud had dried now and it fell off them like dust.

5

WE TOOK THE same path back. When we reached the pile of sleepers, Pavel and I picked one up and slung it across our shoulders. Pavel walked in front and I walked behind. Kyabine and Sifra took one too and we all walked back to the camp.

Kyabine and Sifra walked ahead. Suddenly, Pavel and I started running. We passed them. We heard Kyabine shouting: 'Sifra! Sifra!'

The sleeper was cutting into our shoulders but we kept running. Soon we heard the ragged breathing of Kyabine and Sifra just behind us. They were getting closer. Just as they were about to overtake us, Pavel and I moved to opposite sides of the path, so our sleeper blocked their way. But they found a way around this. They left the path and now they were running alongside us in the grass field. We stared at each other, eyes bulging from the effort. The sleepers were weighing ever more heavily on our shoulders. For an instant we were equal, running at the same speed. Then

17

Kyabine and Sifra sneaked ahead. But Kyabine put his foot in a hole. He collapsed and we had time to see their sleeper flying over Kyabine's head. We slowed down now because we were sure of our victory. We lifted up the sleeper to give our shoulders a rest.

But suddenly Kyabine surged past us on our right. He was carrying the sleeper on his own, still running in the field. His mouth was wide open and he was staring straight ahead, his expression serious and tense. He hadn't given up. Pavel and I started to run again, but not too fast, just fast enough to stay alongside Kyabine, and to taunt him. His face was a picture of pain. While it was true he was the biggest and strongest of us all, running while carrying a sleeper single-handed was too tough: he stood no chance. He slowed down and finally he threw the sleeper on the ground and came to a halt.

We had won.

6

AS I'VE SAID, the camp was situated at the edge of a pine wood. At the end of the winter when we were still living in huts, we'd all been ordered to make tents. We used the tarpaulin that we'd stolen from the factory in Galicia to make ours. It was spacious and there was enough height at the centre for us to stand upright. Pavel had made a tent pole from a tree branch, taking care to keep the beginnings of the secondary branches. That was pretty clever too, because we could use them to hang up our rifles. They were always dry and within easy reach, and they didn't bother us while we were sleeping.

We dropped the railway sleepers outside the tent. Pavel left for the camp with Kyabine. They returned with a wooden crate that we placed upside down between the sleepers so we could play dice.

Kyabine had got another bit of tobacco from Sifra.

He managed to roll half a dozen thin cigarettes. He lit one and, instead of keeping the rest, put them on top of the wooden crate. He wanted to gamble them at dice against Pavel. 'I'm going to clean you out,' he boasted.

Pavel replied: 'Play!'

Kyabine threw the dice, repeating: 'I'm going to clean you out, Pavel.'

Pavel picked up the dice and, looking at the cigarette that dangled between Kyabine's lips, said: 'Good idea to smoke that one.'

'What?' said Kyabine.

Pavel didn't respond. He threw the dice on the crate.

'Hey!' said Kyabine. 'Why did you say that, Pavel?'

Then suddenly he understood. Shaking his head, he answered: 'No, Pavel, *I'm* going to clean *you* out.'

'Play, Kyabine!' said Pavel.

7

DUSK FELL AND there were no more cigarettes on the crate in front of Kyabine. They had all gone over to Pavel's side and now he had taken out his cigarette case and was putting them inside. Kyabine did not look at anyone, least of all Sifra, who had given him the tobacco he'd just lost. Kyabine stared at the top of the wooden crate and looked very surprised.

Pavel put his cigarette case back in his pocket and said to Kyabine: 'You simply didn't deserve to win.'

Kyabine looked at Pavel. 'What?'

And Pavel repeated: 'You didn't deserve to win.'

Kyabine was nonplussed. He didn't understand what Pavel was getting at. Neither did Sifra or I. Pavel was obviously taking the piss out of Kyabine. We just hadn't yet understood in what way he was taking the piss out of him. In a grave voice, Pavel asked him: 'Have you done one single good thing today to deserve to win?'

'I don't know, Pavel,' Kyabine replied. 'I don't know.'

Pavel continued to stare at him gravely while Kyabine thought about this. Suddenly he asked: 'What about you, Pavel? Have you done something good today?'

Pavel replied: 'It's difficult to talk about the good things you've done.'

'At least tell me one good thing,' said Kyabine.

But Pavel remained silent. Now Kyabine stared at him entreatingly. Sifra and I, too, were curious to find out about Pavel's good deeds. Thankfully we managed to remain serious. Suddenly Pavel said: 'This morning I pissed on a swarm of ants that were trying to eat a caterpillar.'

Kyabine looked at me and Sifra, then he looked at Pavel and he said: 'Huh? What?'

'What do you think, Kyabine? Could the caterpillar defend itself?'

Now Kyabine stared questioningly at me and Sifra.

Pavel explained: 'It was a nice fat caterpillar and it was wriggling around trying to escape those little bastards. So I thought to myself: Pavel, it's time to do a good deed.'

Kyabine slapped his hand on the wooden crate and said: 'I reckon you're having us on.'

Pavel did not reply.

'Yeah, you're having us on,' Kyabine said. 'You shouldn't do that to me.'

As Pavel still didn't say anything, Kyabine demanded: 'Give me some proof!'

Pavel took out his cigarette case and opened it. It was full of cigarettes, some of them the ones he had won from Kyabine. 'This is proof, don't you think?' he said.

'No, that's not proof,' Kyabine replied.

Pavel picked up a cigarette, put the case back in his pocket, lit the cigarette, and said: 'I told you one of my good deeds, Kyabine. Now piss off!'

Kyabine just sat there brooding.

8

SOON AFTER THIS, as it was his turn, Kyabine went to fetch dinner.

He came back and we ate outside the tent in silence. The oil lamp was on top of the crate and it illuminated our faces. We were very comfortable. It had been a brilliant idea to bring the sleepers here. Whatever we did – playing dice or eating meals – there they were, right in front of the tent. If they hadn't been so heavy, we would have taken them everywhere with us.

Kyabine stopped eating. 'Sifra!'

'Yes, Kyabine.'

'Do you believe that story about Pavel's caterpillar?'

Sifra looked embarrassed. He waited before replying. He liked Kyabine, he liked him a lot. Pavel and I liked him too, of course, but we also liked taking the piss out of him. Sifra was more considerate towards him.

In a kind voice, he answered: 'I don't know, Kyabine.'

Kyabine didn't dare ask me what I thought. Anyway, he

knew that I would back Pavel up. He started eating again and suddenly he said: 'I think you talk a lot of crap, Pavel!'

Pavel didn't reply.

'Yes, Pavel, yes, you talk so much crap!' Kyabine said.

Pavel stopped eating. He picked up his cigarette case, opened it and took out a cigarette, which he handed to Kyabine. Kyabine took it from him and put it on the crate in front of him. He thought for a bit and then he asked: 'Why did you give me that?'

'So you'll stop giving me shit.'

Kyabine started to laugh. He looked at the cigarette and said: 'If that's how it works, I'm going to keep giving you shit.'

He was very pleased with himself for being so clever. He looked up at the sky. Then, after a while, he leaned towards Pavel and, to put his cleverness into practice, said to him: 'You talk so much crap, Pavel, that no one believes you any more. You think you're conning me, Pavel, but you're not. Not at all. I don't believe a word of the crap you spout. For a start, show me where you pissed on the ants!'

Pavel calmly picked up his cigarette case, took out a cigarette and placed it in front of Kyabine. Kyabine sat there frozen. He didn't say another word. He hadn't really expected his cleverness to work. What I mean is, he hadn't actually believed that Pavel would give him another cigarette so he would stop giving Pavel shit. He stared at Pavel in surprise.

We could now feel the warmth from the fires that the company had lit outside the tents. The woodsmoke drifted over to us. It was good to smoke a cigarette with that smell in the air.

Kyabine, taking a drag on his, continued to stare at Pavel with that surprised look on his face.

9

THE AIR GREW damp and we went inside the tent. We lay down under our blankets. We spread our coats on top of them because it still got cold at night. The blankets were dirty and Sifra, in his soft woman's voice, suggested we wash them in the pond tomorrow. We all agreed.

Kyabine said: 'If you want, Sifra, I'll wash yours.'

'Why?'

'To pay you back for the tobacco.'

Sifra said in a kind voice, as if he was asking him for a favour: 'I'd rather you gave it back to me, Kyabine.'

Abruptly, Pavel sat up and asked: 'Who's got the watch?'

I remembered that I had it. I passed it to Pavel because it was his turn to sleep with it. Not for the watch itself, since the mechanism was broken, but for the photograph of a woman that was inside it. It was nice to sleep with that photograph. We imagined that it brought us luck. We didn't know why. I reckon, deep down, we didn't really believe it brought us luck. But we liked to think it did.

Pavel, Kyabine and I took turns to sleep with it. But not Sifra. It was hard to understand why. None of us had ever asked him. And yet he was the one who'd taken the watch from the corpse of a cavalry officer in Galicia, along with the boots he was wearing. He wears the boots, I thought to myself, so why doesn't he want to sleep with the photograph in the watch?

One day Pavel said to me that Sifra had perhaps never slept with a woman, so sleeping with the photograph didn't have any meaning for him. Maybe it was that. But I was sure that Kyabine had never slept with a woman either, and that didn't stop him taking his turn with the photograph.

I didn't tell Pavel that I had never slept with a woman either.

Pavel was probably the only one who had.

10

FOR A MOMENT after Pavel touched my arm, I didn't really know what was going on or where I was. Pavel touched my arm again. Now I was awake. We put on our boots, picked up our coats and quietly slipped out of the tent.

The fires were almost burned out. The embers glowed in the night. We put on our coats and left the camp. We walked in silence over to the pile of railway sleepers. From there we went into the field and headed towards the pond.

Pavel crouched down by the edge of the water. I remained standing, as far away as possible. All the same I could hear him sobbing. Sometimes I also heard a faint noise on the surface of the pond. Last night there'd been the sound of the wind, which had drowned out all the other noises.

We went out together every night, Pavel and I, and had done ever since we left the forest. Every night Pavel dreamed that Sifra cut his throat. It was a horrible dream. He woke up in terror. So he needed to get out of the tent and he needed me to go with him. We came here to the pond, or sometimes we stopped at the pile of sleepers. Occasionally, although it was rare, he wept like he was doing tonight, and then he felt better. Sometimes I thought to myself that it was probably in this way, for Pavel, that the winter in the forest continued to live inside him. But neither Pavel nor I understood why Sifra should be the killer in his dreams. Sifra was so gentle and sweet with us, he was such a good comrade.

If it was me who cut his throat every night, I thought, I would be very unhappy. And then it probably wouldn't be me who he needed to come with him to help him calm down.

Pavel's sobs died down.

I remained standing and I looked at the surface of the pond. I would have liked to move closer to Pavel, but I thought it was better to wait until he wanted me to.

I continued to wait, and it seemed to me that Pavel was hardly crying any more and that he now wanted me to go to him. He hadn't made any sign, he hadn't moved or anything, but I sensed that he wanted me with him now. So I went over and crouched down next to him.

He took out his cigarette case, opened it and held it out to me. I took one and we smoked, almost peacefully, as we looked at the pond.

Pavel wasn't crying at all any more. He breathed the

smoke out between his legs. We were nice and warm in our coats and I would have liked to find something to say to console him.

On our way back Pavel took long strides through the grass. He'd opened his coat and it was flapping against his legs. I hadn't thought of anything to say to him on the bank of the pond, and I had given up trying to find the right words.

I just asked him: 'You all right, Pavel?'

'Yeah.'

We reached the pile of sleepers in front of the train tracks and we turned onto the path that led to the camp. The night was still very dark. There was no moon and dawn was still a long way off.

I I

WE HAD TO go on an expedition the next day. We knew about it, because they'd told us in advance, but we'd forgotten. Sergeant Ermakov came to fetch us at dawn. We got dressed and left the camp behind him, dragging our heels.

We hoped we could find a farm quickly, so that we could come back before evening and go to the pond. We didn't like these expeditions. Something bad always happened.

I walked next to Pavel. Nothing on his face betrayed the terrible fear he'd felt during the night. Pavel and I never talked about any of it in the daytime, about his nightmares or our nocturnal outings. I think it was better that way. Though of course, if he'd wanted to talk about it, I would have listened.

Kyabine and Sifra knew nothing about Pavel's nightmares. Perhaps one or the other might have heard us get up in the middle of the night, but they didn't know why. I was the only one who knew and I felt proud of that.

We walked for an hour.

Sergeant Ermakov remained ahead of us the whole time. He tore up stems of grass and chewed them as he walked.

We saw smoke in the distance.

We found a road and spotted a small village. Sergeant Ermakov made us toss away our cigarettes and button up our coats. But below our coats were the German boots worn by Pavel and me, Kyabine's big civilian shoes, and Sifra's cavalry boots. Only our coats and our caps were regulation uniform.

Sergeant Ermakov went into the courtyard of the first house. We waited for him on the road. We weren't allowed to sit down or smoke. And we had to leave our rifles slung over our shoulders.

Sergeant Ermakov knocked at the door, then at the window. A man came out into the courtyard. He was wearing a forest ranger's uniform. They talked for a little while, then went over to the vegetable garden at the foot of the courtyard. The forest ranger started pulling up winter leeks. Sergeant Ermakov helped him by removing the earth that clung to their roots.

The forest ranger looked cheerful as he pulled up the leeks. He knew he was getting off lightly. His garden was full of leeks.

Behind me, Pavel muttered: 'Hey, stick one of those leeks up Ermakov's arse, would you?'

Kyabine started silently laughing, mouth shut tight and shoulders shaking. The forest ranger and the sergeant went back up to the courtyard. The sergeant took out the requisition papers to fill out, but the forest ranger put his hands on the sergeant's, as if to say: no need for a receipt, these leeks are a gift from me to you and the Red Army.

Sergeant Ermakov put the papers back in his pocket and the forest ranger tied up the bundle of leeks with a piece of string. After that he went back into the house and he came back out with a sack of potatoes.

I2

THE SECOND HOUSE was unoccupied. I suggested we go in anyway to take a look around, but Sergeant Ermakov didn't want to. Kyabine carried the bundle of leeks over his shoulder. He smiled every time he looked at Sergeant Ermakov, and you could tell that he was still thinking about what Pavel had said earlier about the leeks and Ermakov's arse.

I was carrying the potatoes. They were from last year, of course, and were starting to sprout. They smelled of old potatoes. They smelled of spring, because it's at this time of year that you sort through them all, throwing away the ones that have sprouted so much that there's hardly any flesh left on them.

There was a pig in the courtyard of the third house. It was digging in the ground with its snout. It lifted its head to look at us when we arrived. Kyabine and I put the leeks and potatoes down on the road. Sergeant Ermakov went into the courtyard alone. He walked past the pig, looked around, and knocked on the door.

A man and a woman came out and they started talking with Ermakov. We could hear what they were saying. The man and the woman had two sons in the Shuyski regiment. They asked if we knew where the Shuyski regiment was at that moment. Sergeant Ermakov shook his head and told them that we didn't know where any of the other regiments were.

Then they talked about a distribution problem, although we couldn't hear the details of what they were saying. Sergeant Ermakov seemed to agree with them, in any case.

Suddenly the woman went back into the house and came out with a chicken. She must have been about to pluck it because it was steaming and dripping with water. But Sergeant Ermakov told them they could keep the chicken because unfortunately we had to take their pig. The woman let the chicken dangle from her hand and the man cried out breathlessly that it had been too hard to feed it all winter for them to let it go now. I wanted to yell at him that, if he wanted, we could tell him all about our winter in the forest and what we had to eat there.

Sergeant Ermakov took a few steps back because the man was yelling louder and louder, and he was looking threatening now. In the meantime the woman had gone to sit on the front doorstep of the house. She put the chicken between her knees and started crying.

Ermakov turned to us.

It was time. Pavel and Sifra went into the courtyard. The man fell silent. His face tensed. His hands started trembling so much that suddenly we felt sorry for him, despite our winter in the forest. His eyes were full of tears. But it was his hands that were unbearable to watch.

Pavel and Sifra walked between the sergeant and the man and went over to the pig. And while they were shoving it out of the courtyard, Sergeant Ermakov kindly asked the man what his sons were called.

13

I CARRIED THE potatoes and Kyabine the leeks. Ahead of us Pavel and Sifra herded the pig. Sergeant Ermakov walked at the back of the procession.

Sometimes, when the pig started slowing down or moving sideways, Pavel would shove it with the butt of his rifle and yell at it: 'Come on, get a move on, Kyabine!'

Or: 'Oh, Kyabine, what the hell are you doing? Keep going straight!'

This made Kyabine laugh.

Behind us, Sergeant Ermakov said nothing. I could tell that he was thinking about the man and woman in the courtyard, and that the memory tormented him. We'd requisitioned food with Ermakov before, and he was always like that. He always acted as if it was his own home that we were raiding. We knew he owned a farm somewhere. At the rate we requisitioned other farms, he must have had the impression that there would be nothing left of his own farm by the time he went home. But what could we do about it?

Without turning around, I asked him what the Shuyski regiment was. He replied that he had no idea. So I asked him why he'd asked those people for the names of their sons, who were in that regiment. He told me to advance.

I advanced. But I did so ever more sadly. The sadness was stronger than me. It was because of the smell of the potatoes slung over my shoulder. It didn't evoke anything precise, that smell. Not one specific event, in any case. What it evoked was just a distant time.

In the end I started feeling really low.

I lengthened my stride to catch up with Pavel and walked beside him. I needed to feel him next to me. I didn't want to tell him how sad I was, I just wanted him beside me. But he was busy herding the pig. He didn't have time to pay any attention to me. He started talking to the pig as if it were Kyabine again. Behind me, I heard Kyabine laugh. That gave me an idea.

I slowed down, and when Kyabine had caught up with me I offered to swap my sack of potatoes for his bundle of leeks. He gestured sideways with his head at his empty shoulder. I slung the sack over it and was about to take the leeks from him. But he made a sign to say that he was fine like that, that he could carry it all.

In front of us, Pavel shouted at the pig: 'Come on, Kyabine, are you going to advance or what?'

Laughing, Kyabine called out: 'You're the pig, Pavel!'

Behind us, Sergeant Ermakov barked: 'For God's sake, just shut your mouths, all of you!'

14

BY THE TIME we got back to the camp, the morning was over and the sun was high in the sky. It was lunchtime. The kitchen had been built in the pine forest. There was a stone hearth and some trestles with planks resting on them. The saucepans, buckets and ladles were hung from nails in the trees. Behind this you could see the company office, which we had built under a canopy of branches.

The cook was so happy that we'd brought him back a pig that he gave us extra portions, along with a good pinch of powdered tea, which Sifra held in the hollow of his palm, like some precious treasure. It was rare to have tea there.

We asked Sergeant Ermakov if he wanted to come and drink it with us. He replied: 'Don't worry about me.'

We didn't understand what he meant by that. We went to our tent, Pavel lit a fire, and we ate our food and listened to the boiling water whistle in our kettle.

We quickly finished eating so we could enjoy our tea.

But we had a problem. It happened every time we

managed to get some tea. What the cook had given us was, as usual, only enough to make about half a cup of real tea. And there were four of us.

So, if we added a lot of water, the tea wouldn't have much taste. If we didn't add much, it would taste like real tea but there would only be enough for one or two mouthfuls each. Sometimes we spent a long time discussing this before we made the tea.

This time there was no dispute and it went a bit faster. All four of us agreed that it would be better to make a small amount of tea. That way, it would be nice and strong, the way we liked it. We kept it in our mouths until it was tepid. Only then did we swallow it. It didn't last long, and as soon as we'd swallowed it we all wished we could go back one minute in time.

Barely had we finished drinking that tea before we became nostalgic for it.

But, all the same, it was better than no tea at all.

15

WE PUT OUT the fire. We rolled up our blankets, tucked them under our arms and set off for the pond. When we reached the pile of sleepers, just as we were about to go into the field, Pavel said: 'We can't go to the pond that way any more.'

We stared at him. We didn't understand. He pointed out the path we'd made by tramping down the grass and explained to us that if we kept taking that path we would end up showing the way to the pond to the rest of the company. And if that happened . . . farewell pond and farewell tranquillity.

We climbed onto the railway track and followed it for half a mile or so. Then, leaving gaps of several hundred feet between us, we went into the field. Spaced out like that, we had more chance of finding the pond because we'd cover more ground than if we all walked together.

The grass was so tall that we couldn't see where we were going. We advanced, each of us alone, solitary, as if none of us had ever had any comrades. I am saying this for all four of us because I feel certain that Pavel, Kyabine and Sifra felt the same way I did as we moved blindly forward through that field. That was why, after a while, we started yelling at each other at the tops of our voices. We heard Kyabine calling out: 'Pavel! Sifra! Benia!'

And we called out in turn: 'Kyabine! Kyabine! Kyabine!'

'Oh lads, I'm over here!' Kyabine shouted.

'You're over there, Kyabine!' we replied.

And Kyabine in his booming voice: 'Yes, I'm here!'

'So, have you found it?'

And in the same thunderous voice, Kyabine answered: 'Not yet, but I'm here.'

It was better like that. We continued to advance blindly, but the sound of our voices did us good. We had comrades again. Birds flew up in front of us. One of those types of birds that nest in grass.

Suddenly Pavel yelled out: 'Kyabine!'

'Yes, Pavel, what?' Kyabine replied.

And Pavel yelled as loud as he could: 'You big Uzbeki idiot!'

Kyabine's laughter echoed above the tall grass.

We continued moving forward and suddenly we heard Sifra: 'I found it!'

'Where?'

'Over here!'

We converged on him. He was smiling as he watched us arrive. He was very happy that he was the one who'd found it.

The pond was calm. There was no wind.

We approached the water. We could see the bottom of the pond today.

We spread our blankets on the ground and lay on top of them. The sun was hot, and soon we took off our boots and our coats and folded up the coats so we could rest our heads on them. All of us except for Sifra, who remained sitting and disassembled his rifle, carefully lining the pieces up on his blanket.

I lay on my side and closed my eyes. The air smelled of the pond, of mud and grass, and everything was peaceful.

I've already said that this was a precious place.

I never grow weary of saying that.

'Please, Benia, give me some tobacco!'

That was Kyabine, of course.

I was about to say no so that he would have to beg me. But then I remembered the sack of potatoes that he'd slung over his shoulder and carried for me while also carrying the bundle of leeks.

I sat up and gave him what he needed to roll a cigarette. He couldn't believe it. He stared rapturously at the tobacco. I lay back down and closed my eyes.

When I woke up, there was no one else near me. Kyabine was in the middle of the pond, carrying Sifra on his shoulders. Sifra was hanging onto Kyabine's hair because he was afraid of the water.

Pavel was sitting on the opposite bank, on the other side of the pond. When he noticed that I was awake, he stood up and came over to me.

So did Kyabine and Sifra. They waded back to the bank, with Sifra clinging tightly to Kyabine's hair until the very last moment. Not until Kyabine was standing on the sand did he let go.

We washed our blankets.

We soaked them in the water then rubbed them with sand. We rinsed them and then rubbed them with sand again.

We rinsed them one last time and spread them out on the grass. The sun was so hot that steam rose from them.

16

WE WENT BACK to the camp with our clean, dry blankets. Near the pile of sleepers we bumped into Yassov, the hand sculptor, just as he was stepping over the railway tracks.

He accompanied us back to the camp. He told us that he'd been to sell his hands to the men in Kossarenko's company. They were camped on the plain too, but on the other side of the train tracks. Sometimes we could see the smoke from their fires in the distance.

'Did you sell any?' Kyabine asked Yassov.

'Yes, one,' Yassov replied.

'What did you get?' Kyabine asked.

'This!'

And he took half a dozen ready-rolled cigarettes from his pocket. They were thin, but they were cigarettes all the same. Kyabine stared at them enviously. Yassov put them back in his pocket and said: 'We're not going to stay here much longer.'

'What?' said Pavel. 'What are you talking about?'

47

'We're going to leave this place soon. Kossarenko told me.'

'How soon?' asked Pavel.

'A few more days and we'll be gone.'

We believed Yassov. This was bad news. We continued walking in silence. Then I asked Yassov if he knew where we were going. He didn't. We would be leaving soon – that was all he'd been able to learn from Kossarenko.

When we got back to the camp, we were sombre and silent. How many days did we have left to go to the pond and peacefully play dice outside our tent whenever we felt like it?

We took our blankets into the tent and went for a walk around the camp, mess tins in hand, while we waited for the cook to bang his ladle against his bucket. Our mood was still gloomy after the news about our imminent departure.

Outside the tents, men lit fires. They boiled water in the hope that there would be tea tonight. Some of them played dice outside their tents. There were a few men that we knew better than the others. We used to chat with them sometimes. We walked up to them to watch them play.

We asked them if they'd heard the news that we would be leaving soon. They told us that everyone had heard the news.

And where are we going? we asked them. No one knew.

Pavel gestured to us. It was nearly time. We walked closer to the pine forest. But not too close because the cook didn't like it when everyone crowded around the kitchen before he had given the signal.

Suddenly we heard the ladle bang against the bucket.

We rushed over to the kitchen. We were the first ones there and we held out our mess tins. But we didn't see what they were putting in the tins because we were looking past the kitchen at some young lads sitting under a pine tree outside the company office. There were five or six of them. The oldest one was younger than Sifra. They were all eating out of the same saucepan. Most of them were dressed like peasants. Three officers – Kaliakine, our commander, Lieutenant Dymov and Sergeant Ermakov – were leaning against the company office, pensively watching them eat.

'Who are they?' we asked the cook.

'They came up the train tracks,' the cook replied.

'And?'

'They want to enlist.'

Before we went away, we asked him if there was any tea tonight. No, there wasn't, he replied. We asked him if there might be any just for us. But the answer was still no. That bastard – he'd already forgotten that we were the ones who'd brought him the pig.

We walked back to the tent with our mess tins. All of those men boiling water for tea would soon be disappointed. They'd be drinking plain hot water instead. As we were passing, we called out to them: 'Hurry up, there's tea tonight!'

17

IT WAS KYABINE'S turn to sleep with the watch. Pavel handed it to him and he kissed it lovingly. We really liked it when he did that. He knew it, and his kisses became ever more passionate. Sometimes Pavel told him that if the woman in the photograph had known that a big Uzbeki idiot kissed her like that every third evening, it would have put her off men for ever. Kyabine asked him what the hell he knew about it. Pavel replied that he knew.

Finally Kyabine delicately placed the watch under his blanket and lay down. I asked him if he would let me have the watch tonight in return for a cigarette.

'What?' he said.

I asked him again. Would he agree to let me have his turn with the watch if I gave him a cigarette? He thought about this for a moment and then asked: 'How many would you give me?'

He'd heard me say one, of course. I wasn't going to let him rip me off. 'One, Kyabine,' I repeated. 'One cigarette.'

'Two,' he said.

'You can keep the watch, Kyabine,' I told him.

He realised I wasn't going to back down. He seemed to hesitate, then he raised himself up on one elbow. I took out a cigarette and handed it to him. He kissed the watch one last time before giving it to me.

'And who gets to sleep with it tomorrow?' he asked.

I replied that we would go back to our normal rota tomorrow, which meant that it was my turn.

'Ah!' he sighed, disappointed.

He remained raised up on his elbow. I was afraid he was going to change his mind. I put the watch in my pocket, blew out the oil lamp and lay down.

It was a pleasant feeling to have a clean blanket. I said this to Sifra because it had been his idea to wash them, but he didn't reply. He was already asleep.

I lay there with my eyes wide open.

I could smell the oil from the lamp and I thought about our winter in the forest.

18

WHEN PAVEL WOKE me in the night, I accidentally knocked
Kyabine's leg as I was getting out of bed. He looked up and
said: 'What are you doing?'

We didn't answer. I tucked my coat under my arm. But
Kyabine wouldn't let it go.

'What are you doing? Where are you going?'

'Go back to sleep, Kyabine!' I told him.

'Huh?'

'Everything's fine. Just go back to sleep.'

We left the tent and rushed out of the camp before Kyabine had time to think of getting up and following us.

That night, Pavel didn't want to go to the pond. He
stopped at the pile of sleepers and sat down on them. I left
him in peace. I climbed onto the train tracks and walked on
the ballast, slowly, because I didn't want to go too far away.

Sometimes, during the daytime, I thought about what
I might say to Pavel to console him. And of course I found
things to say. But at night, when it was just the two of us,

either I didn't dare say those things or I couldn't remember them. So sometimes I was afraid that Pavel would think he was unlucky having a comrade like me. What good did it do him to wake me up and bring me with him if I never said a word to console him?

I made a U-turn and walked back to the sleepers. But when I got to where Pavel was sitting, I just kept going because I had the impression that he still wanted to be alone a little longer.

I would have liked to light a cigarette but I preferred to wait and smoke one with him.

I walked another hundred yards or so and then I turned back again. When I reached him, I sensed that he was feeling better, so I asked if he was all right.

He nodded. I sat on the sleeper facing him and offered him a cigarette. I could see glimmers in the distance – almost certainly Kossarenko's camp. They still had fires lit at that time of night.

I held back from doing what I had been planning to do since the previous night. I waited until we had finished our cigarettes. And even after we'd thrown the butts on the train tracks and I was watching their glowing ends fade, I continued to hesitate.

Then at last I did it. I took the watch from my pocket

and handed it to Pavel. Because it was so dark, he asked me what it was.

'Take it,' I said. 'It's the watch.'

19

PAVEL CALMED DOWN and we went back to the camp. He'd accepted the watch and I was proud of myself for having had that idea to console him. We both knew that the watch didn't really bring us luck and that we weren't really sleeping with the woman inside it. As I've said, we just liked to imagine those things. All the same, when it was our turn to have it, we were always very happy to put it in our pocket for the night. And Pavel must have felt that way now. Two nights running with her – he must have been doubly happy. I didn't regret the cigarette it had cost me. In fact, if Kyabine had insisted, I'd have given him more for it. Thankfully he didn't realise how much I needed the watch.

The path was wide enough for us to walk side by side. This was the path we'd run along when we were racing with the railway sleepers. That gave me an idea for a conversation, so I said: 'We beat Kyabine good and proper, in that race.'

'What?'

'It was here that we had the race,' I reminded him.

'Oh . . . yeah.'

'We beat him good and proper, eh?'

It wasn't as cold as the night before. I was sleepy. I felt good because we were headed back to the camp and I would soon be able to go to sleep. I hoped we could sneak into the tent without waking Kyabine.

I was dog-tired but everything was fine. I was happy that I'd had the idea of the watch, and I was happy that I'd soon be back in bed. Then suddenly everything stopped being fine because I started wondering again: what if I took Sifra's place in Pavel's dream? What if it was me who cut his throat? What would happen then? Would Pavel still want me to go with him at night? I knew the answer to that last question. Pavel would never say to me: 'I dreamed that you cut my throat – let's go outside. I want you to come with me because I need you by my side.' No, he would probably ask Kyabine or Sifra instead. And I understood that.

When we reached the tent, I felt sad and worried. Pavel was feeling better. He fell asleep straight away with the watch.

I lay there with my eyes open.

I was sleeping next to Sifra. I heard him breathing and may God have mercy on me but at that moment I hoped with all my strength that it would always be him who held the knife in Pavel's dreams.

20

SERGEANT ERMAKOV POKED his head through the gap in our tent. He looked at each of us in turn. We knew he couldn't be here to take us on an expedition, because we'd gone with him only yesterday. So we asked him what he wanted. 'Get out of there!' he ordered.

The sun had risen and we should have been up, but we were nice and warm under our blankets.

'Let us sleep!' Pavel groaned.

'Get out of there!' Sergeant Ermakov repeated.

We didn't move. Sergeant Ermakov grew angry. He started kicking the tent. So we had to get up and go outside before he tore it.

The camp was shrouded in mist. The sun was still hidden behind the pine forest. Next to Sergeant Ermakov was one of the young lads we'd seen eating outside the company office the previous day. He had a blanket draped over his shoulders. Beneath that he wore a sailor's shirt and a jacket.

Pavel sat on a railway sleeper to put on his boots.

'He's going to be with you,' said Sergeant Ermakov.

We stared at Sergeant Ermakov in astonishment. Then Kyabine, Sifra and I turned to Pavel, who had stopped in the middle of putting his boots on. Silently we asked him to say something to Sergeant Ermakov. He seemed to understand this and told the sergeant: 'We're not going to take him. You, Sergeant, are going to kick him out of the army and send him back to his mother.'

The kid looked down at his peasant's boots. Sergeant Ermakov remained calm and said: 'You'll have to tell him how things work around here, the organisation and all that.'

As he finished putting on his boots, Pavel said: 'We're not going to tell him anything because we don't want him.' At that, Pavel looked up at us and asked: 'Eh? Do we want him?'

We weren't as bold as Pavel in front of Sergeant Ermakov. None of us said a word, but it was still an eloquent response. Sergeant Ermakov sat on the sleeper facing Pavel and said: 'You've got a bloody big mouth.'

Pavel pulled apart the opening of the tent. 'Look, Ermakov,' he said. 'You can't fit five of us in there.'

Sergeant Ermakov did not look inside the tent. It was a good thing he didn't, really, because there was plenty of

59

room for five people in there. He said calmly: 'We're going to be leaving this place soon.'

Then he stood up and left.

The kid continued staring at his peasant's boots.

21

WE PREFERRED TO stay in the camp that morning. We played dice. We didn't gamble. The dice kept falling off the wooden crate. We didn't speak. We took turns to throw the dice. We hardly bothered keeping score. The kid sat there and watched us. He was sitting on the end of Kyabine and Sifra's sleeper. He still had the blanket over his shoulders. We had nothing against him. We just didn't want him to be there.

When the kid got up to go and take a piss, Kyabine waited until he'd moved out of earshot and then asked why we weren't going to the pond. Pavel said it was risky, showing it to the kid, because Sergeant Ermakov might change his mind and put him in a different tent. And if he did that, then we could wave goodbye to the tranquillity of the pond.

I thought about this and said to Pavel: 'Yeah, but seeing as we're going to be leaving soon anyway, we might not get to go there at all any more.'

Pavel admitted this was true.

'And I don't think Ermakov is going to change his mind,' I added.

The kid returned. He'd taken the blanket off his shoulders and was holding it under his arm. Sifra told him to put the blanket in the tent.

The kid stepped over the wooden crate and went into the tent. We started playing again. In a low voice Kyabine asked: 'So are we going to the pond?'

Pavel threw the dice.

22

KYABINE AND THE kid went to fetch the meal. The kid did not have a mess tin or any cutlery. But when he came back, he had everything he needed: a mess tin, a half-pint mug, a knife and a spoon.

We ate and smoked. We played dice for a bit and then we questioned the kid. And this is what he told us: he was from Vsevolozhsk, near Lake Ladoga. He'd taken the train from St Petersburg. He'd travelled on a running board all the way to Mogilev. Then from Mogilev to Voronezh. That was where he'd been told where to find part of the Third Army: us.

At the Cheka office he'd been given the clothes he was wearing, plus some underwear and a regulation blanket. He'd been told to wait for other new volunteers and to follow the railway tracks to our camp.

We asked him if he'd ever held a rifle before. Yes, he said, a hunting rifle. We asked him his name. He was called Kouzma Evdokim. I asked him how many times he'd been hunting. Just once, he said. Kyabine asked him if he had any tobacco. No, but he did have some tea left.

We lit the fire, boiled some water and prepared the tea. This time we didn't have to worry about how many cups we would make. There was plenty: enough for a whole kettle's worth. The tea tasted bitter. It wasn't as good as the tea we'd been given before. But, all the same, we drank every drop of it.

After that, we went for a walk around the camp. The Evdokim kid came with us. We still had the bitter taste of his tea in our mouths. We stopped outside Yassov's tent. He'd copied our idea of putting a railway sleeper outside his tent. He was sitting at one end of it and sculpting a hand. Five or six finished hands were lined up next to him on the sleeper. He glanced up at us then continued to work.

We still didn't want his hands. But it was interesting to watch him sculpt.

23

WE WALKED UP the railway tracks and just as we were about to enter the field and head to the pond, Pavel hesitated. Then he signalled that we should continue along the tracks. It was a shame. Sometimes Pavel was overly cautious. I felt sure that Ermakov wouldn't change his mind about the kid now and put him in another tent.

We walked for an hour and finally reached a station. The inside was empty: no chairs or tables remained. The floor was covered with printed pages. There was a dry turd in one corner. Kyabine threw it out of the window. We sat down on the floor and played dice. I lent Kyabine some tobacco. He rolled one cigarette and smoked it, and he gambled with the rest of the tobacco. He swore to Sifra that he was going to win and pay him back what he owed.

The Evdokim kid watched us play for a while then he went away and we forgot about him. The station was full of smoke. We threw the dice on the papers that covered the floor.

Occasionally clouds floated above the station. The sunlight came and went.

Suddenly I said: 'Where's the kid?'

No one answered.

It was my turn to play. I threw. I counted my points and Pavel picked up the dice.

I got up and went out. The Evdokim kid was sitting there on the platform, his back to the station wall. He was writing in a notebook with a grey cardboard cover. When he saw me, he closed the book and looked embarrassed.

'So!' I said.

He lowered his eyes and started fiddling with the corners of the notebook's cover. I stood there a little longer in the doorframe and then I went back into the station and, as I sat down, I announced that the kid was writing something in a notebook.

It was Kyabine's turn to throw the dice. He rolled them around in his hand.

'What's he writing?' Pavel asked.

'Dunno.'

Suddenly Pavel turned towards the door and said in a loud voice: 'Write to your mother that Kyabine is a big Uzbeki idiot!'

'Don't write that to her!' Kyabine said, laughing.

66

Then he lifted his hand, ready to throw the dice. But he paused and yelled out: 'Write to her that I'm going to score more points than Pavel!'

Only then did he throw. He quickly counted his points and picked up the dice. But it was my turn. I tried to grab them from his hand. But he kept his fist so tightly shut that it was impossible. 'What are you doing, Kyabine?' I asked.

Kyabine giggled and said: 'Don't bother me!'

He threw the dice again and used his big fist to threaten anyone who tried to pick them up.

'I'm going to play until I've scored more points than Pavel. I want the kid to write that to his mother.'

I turned to the door and said: 'You should write that Kyabine is a cheat!'

Kyabine picked up the dice in one hand and used his other hand to hold my mouth shut. Then he threw again, counted the points, and shouted: 'All right, you can write it now!'

He let go of my mouth, put his hands behind his neck, leaned back against the station wall and roared triumphantly: 'Oh, Pavel!'

24

THE SUNLIGHT CONTINUED to dim and brighten. The sky grew overcast, almost as dark as night, and then suddenly we heard a crack of thunder. The Evdokim kid came back into the station and sat with us. We closed the door and the window and we waited for the storm to end. Sifra lay down and fell asleep. When he was asleep like that, you'd have guessed he was the same age as the kid.

This was not a precious place like the pond but at least it sheltered us from the storm. With the door and the window closed, it felt like being inside a house.

The Evdokim kid played with the dice. Pavel and I tried joking around with him. Pavel asked him if he'd written that Kyabine was a big Uzbeki idiot and I asked him if he'd written that Kyabine was a cheat. He didn't answer us. He just gave us a shy look and continued to play with the dice.

Kyabine, who had not been listening to what we were saying but had heard his name spoken, asked us: 'What are you two talking about?'

'Nothing, Kyabine,' I said.

'It wasn't nothing,' Kyabine insisted. 'You said my name.'

Then he addressed the kid: 'What did they say?'

The Evdokim kid was increasingly intimidated. Anyone would have been, in his place. He tried to concentrate on the dice because he didn't know what to say to Kyabine.

The storm moved away. I got up and went out. The rain had flattened the grass and the air smelled good. It smelled of earth and wet grass. The sky above the station was blue, and towards the east it was grey. A bit further off, where the storm was, it was black.

I went back into the station. We woke Sifra and walked back to the camp. I almost fell when I was walking on the train tracks. They were slippery from all the rain. Kyabine saw me. He climbed up on a rail and tried to do better than me. As he was about to succeed, I pushed him and then ran off laughing.

25

JUST BEFORE WE reached the pile of sleepers, Pavel said we could go to the pond. He'd decided there wasn't really much risk that Ermakov would put the kid in another tent.

The pond seemed different to us, after the rain. The water was darker. There was something strange about it, as if it had become deeper. And all around it was different because of the storm. Everything looked new and different. The bank was furrowed with lots of little grooves where the water had streamed through, and all around – and as far as the eye could see – the grass lay flat, soaked by the rain.

Above the pond the sky was blue, as it had been above the station, but its reflection in the water didn't look very blue. The air was transparent.

The day was coming to an end.

We approached the water.

The Evdokim kid was already there. He was putting his hands in the water. For him, this was the first time he'd seen the pond. He couldn't tell how new it looked after the storm.

We smelled the mud as we drew closer to the water. We didn't say anything. I held my rifle by its barrel, the butt leaning on my shoulder, and I lifted my head to sniff the indefinable smell of evening.

A fish jumped from the middle of the pond and Kyabine pointed at where it had appeared. We watched that part of the water to see if it would jump out again.

26

WE'D FORGOTTEN THE dice in the station. We didn't try to figure out who was to blame. We just knew that we'd have to go and find them as soon as we could, before anyone else found them.

The tent was big enough for five. The Evdokim kid wasn't used to our oil lamp, though, and the smoke hurt his eyes.

Kyabine was kicking up a fuss about the watch. I think, in reality, he was just pretending not to understand that it was my turn to have it tonight. 'I bought your turn from you last night,' I reminded him.

'Yeah,' he said, 'but that means it's my turn again now.'

'Stop it, Kyabine,' I replied. 'Stop trying to mess me around. It doesn't mean that at all.'

Finally I asked Pavel: 'Does it, Pavel?'

And Pavel calmly backed me up: 'Kyabine, you know perfectly well how it works.'

Kyabine gave up. He lay down under his blanket and didn't say another word.

But the problem was that Pavel still had the watch with him from the previous night. And neither of us wanted Kyabine to ask why Pavel had it, when I was the one who'd bought his turn. Pavel pretended to reach down for his cigarette case and instead he took out the watch and slipped it under the blanket to me. Nobody saw.

I wondered what the Evdokim kid made of all this. Suddenly Kyabine sat up and said: 'I shouldn't have sold you my turn.'

Seriously, what could the Evdokim kid be thinking about all of this?

I turned off the lamp.

27

PAVEL WOKE ME up and we sneaked out of the tent without waking anyone else. We didn't go to the pond that night either. It had rained so much during the storm that we risked getting wet up to our waists if we tried to cross the field. And how could we dry ourselves afterward?

We went and sat on the sleepers, next to the railway tracks. I waited for Pavel to sit and then I sat on the sleeper just below his. It was a good spot. I was very close to him – I could see his boots on my sleeper – but I wasn't bothering him by looking at him. He had me right beside him and I could wait for his terror to go away without disturbing him. I wouldn't have to wonder when it was the right moment to move closer to him.

It was a clear night. The storm had cleaned up the sky. The stars shone all the way to the horizon, as far as the eye could see.

I'd seen this kind of sky once before, one night in the forest.

Pavel's stove worked perfectly and it was safe too: we were never afraid of our hut catching fire. I've already told you that. But what I didn't say is that the fireplace was very narrow, so we had to feed it with fuel all the time. That wasn't a problem during the day, but at night it was a big problem. How could we arrange things to keep the stove roaring so we wouldn't all freeze to death at night? We used the military method. We divided the night into four parts and each of us took turns to watch the stove. In the evening we stocked up on wood inside the hut so nobody would have to put on their coat and their boots and go out into the cold. But one night we ran out. And it was my turn to watch the fire. So I put on my boots and my coat and I went to fetch some wood from our stockpile. And that's the point of my story: it was that night in the forest that I saw this sky.

Behind me, Pavel was silent. He moved occasionally and I heard his sleeper creak against the others.

Perhaps he wanted me to speak now?

I suggested we go to the station to pick up the dice. I thought it would give us something to do and help him forget his nightmare. But I had spoken too soon. If we brought the dice back, we'd have them on us tomorrow morning when we woke, and how would we explain that to the others? Anyway, Pavel didn't say anything. I don't think he'd been listening. I went back to gazing at the sky.

But I wasn't thinking any more about the sky I'd seen in the forest.

Pavel was still silent.

And then suddenly I was seized again by that fear that one day I would take Sifra's place in Pavel's dreams.

And Pavel's silence went on so long that I started thinking: it's already happened, I've already replaced Sifra, I was the one who was holding the knife in his dream and he doesn't dare tell me.

Without turning around, I quietly called out: 'Pavel!'

'What?'

A very brief pause and then: 'Was it still Sifra in your dream?'

'Why?'

'Tell me it was still him.'

'Yes, it was him.'

I relaxed. I felt confident again. And that confidence felt so good that I wanted more. Expecting that he would yell at me straight away for asking such a question, for having even thought it, I asked him: 'Pavel, if it was me who did it . . . instead of Sifra, I mean . . . what would we do?'

I couldn't see him, but I could tell that he was thinking.

So instead of yelling at me straight away for even thinking it, which is what I'd hoped for, instead of that, he was thinking about the possibility of it happening one day. I felt awful.

'I don't know,' he said.

'It doesn't matter, Pavel,' I lied. 'Forget it.'

28

WE GOT UP very early to go and fetch the dice from the station.

We saw them as soon as we opened the door. They were stacked up on top of each other in the middle of the room. Kyabine grabbed them and started juggling them in his hand. I sat in a corner and tried to sleep because I was tired from my nocturnal outing with Pavel. I didn't fall asleep, but it did me good to be able to close my eyes for a little while. When I opened them the station was empty. Everybody had left. I got up and went out onto the platform.

Sifra and the Evdokim kid were sitting against the station wall. Kyabine was crouched in front of them. His coat was spread out on the ground, and all the pieces of his rifle were lined up on it. He was teaching the Evdokim kid. Kyabine started reassembling the rifle until Sifra said: 'Wait!'

'Wait for what?' Kyabine asked.

Sifra, in a gentle voice, said: 'Show him that again.'

'Why?'

'You're going too fast, Kyabine.'

Kyabine picked up the hammer spring again and slowly put it back in place.

'That's better,' Sifra said. 'Don't go any faster than that.'

I spotted Pavel far off in the field. I walked down the platform and joined him. We walked together for a while. When we came back, the rifle was reassembled and Kyabine was asking Sifra to show the kid what he could do. 'Come on, Sifra,' he was saying, 'please do it!'

Sifra smiled at Kyabine.

'Show him, Sifra!' Kyabine pleaded.

I understood what he was talking about and I helped Kyabine convince Sifra to do it.

'Yeah, he's right, Sifra. You should show him!'

Finally Sifra picked up his rifle and completely disassembled it, carefully placing each piece in front of him in a precise order. He always put the pieces in the same order. You'll see why. When Sifra had all the pieces lined up, Kyabine said to the Evdokim kid: 'Now watch this!'

He got to his feet, stood behind Sifra and put his huge hands over Sifra's eyes. Sifra groped with his hands for the first piece to his right and, as soon as he touched it, the show began.

It happened very fast. He reassembled the rifle blind,

more quickly than any of us could do it even when we could see what we were doing. Nobody in the company had as much skill or speed as Sifra when it came to reassembling a rifle. Maybe nobody in the whole Third Army did.

It was over. The rifle was in one piece again. Kyabine removed his hands from Sifra's eyes and he looked at the astonished expression on the Evdokim kid's face.

29

AFTER WITNESSING SIFRA'S demonstration, the Evdokim kid went back into the station. We stayed on the platform, doing nothing. We were silent, each of us lost in his thoughts. I was thinking that the Evdokim kid wasn't really bothering us. Or not as much as we'd feared he would at the beginning, anyway. He followed us around, whatever we did, and barely spoke. I knew he found us intimidating.

Just then Pavel said that before going to the pond we could try crossing the field to see where it led. I poked my head around the station door. The Evdokim kid was writing in his notebook. He looked up at me and I told him that we were going.

We walked down the platform and went into the field. We didn't have to find the pond today, so we walked together. We had taken off our coats and slung them over our shoulders. We were using our rifles as scythes to cut down the grass.

I stopped, turned to the side and took a piss. While I was

doing that, I thought about Pavel's caterpillar because there were lots of insects in the grass. I tried to look for a caterpillar being eaten by ants. There wasn't one. I re-buttoned my trousers and looked up at the sky. Some birds were flying towards us. They were flying quite low and I had the feeling they were ducks. I ran back to the others, yelling that there was a flock of ducks that was going to pass over us. They stopped and turned to look at them. We all held our rifles and when the ducks flew over us, we fired. Then we started running as we reloaded our rifles. We fired again and ran again. We shouted furiously at the ducks, reloaded, and fired. Our coats, slung over our shoulders, got in the way of all our movements. Soon the ducks were a long way ahead of us, but we continued shouting and running after them like madmen, until we reached the road.

We tossed our coats and our rifles in the ditch and we lay down on the road to get our breath back.

When I sat up again, the Evdokim kid was coming out of the field. He sat down with us and asked: 'Did you get any of them?'

For a moment nobody answered him. Then Sifra said: 'No, we had no chance.'

So he must have been wondering why we fired so many shots. Pavel, still lying on the road, took out his cigarette

82

case and offered one to each of us. The Evdokim kid didn't want one. Pavel put the case away. He lit his cigarette and said to the kid: 'So you're writing to your mother?'

The kid looked surprised. 'Oh, no!' he said.

'Who are you writing to, then?' asked Pavel.

The kid hesitated, then said: 'Nobody.'

Pavel rolled onto his side and put his elbow on the road, resting his temple on one hand. 'What the hell!' he said.

All of a sudden he sat up and stared down the road. In the distance a horse and carriage had appeared from around a bend. A man was walking beside the horse, holding its bridle. Pavel continued to stare at the carriage. He stood up, went over to the ditch and grabbed his rifle, and then calmly walked in front of the horse. When he was close to it, the man brought the horse to a halt and held out his hand to Pavel. Pavel put the rifle over his shoulder and shook the man's hand.

We couldn't hear anything from where we were. They were talking together for quite a long time. Suddenly the man pulled on the horse's bridle and tried to turn it around to head back up the road from where he'd come. Pavel took a step back, grabbed his rifle and aimed it at the man, who let go of the bridle.

83

30

WE CROSSED THE field back towards the station. Kyabine wanted to ride the horse first. He held on tight to the creature's mane and stared straight ahead. He looked very serious. He made a few attempts to stand up in the stirrups so he could see farther ahead. But each time he almost lost his balance. Sifra was holding the horse's bridle and the Evdokim kid was carrying Kyabine's rifle and coat.

All of a sudden Kyabine shouted, as though it was something extraordinary: 'I see the station!'

And then, as if spotting the railway station had been the objective of this little horse ride, he called out: 'Stop, Sifra!'

Sifra brought the horse to a stop and Kyabine passed one leg over the animal's hindquarters. He slid down to the ground and took hold of the bridle. 'Your turn, Sifra!' he said.

Sifra handed his rifle to the Evdokim kid and I helped him up onto the horse. Sifra started to tremble. I held his ankle for as long as I could. Then, gently, I let go, and he climbed on top of the horse.

'Are you all right?' Kyabine asked. 'Holding on tight?'

Sifra whispered yes.

Kyabine pulled on the bridle and the horse started to walk. Sifra gripped the horse's mane with all his strength and begged Kyabine to go more slowly.

So Kyabine slowed down and Sifra carefully sat up on the horse. Finally he turned to us and smiled.

And let me tell you, at that moment, I looked at the confident smile on Sifra's face, because Kyabine was leading the horse at the right speed. And I watched Kyabine's slow, reassuring gait, and Pavel was there too, walking next to me, and suddenly I was filled with emotion because each one of us was in his place and also because it seemed to me in that instant that each of us was far away from the winter in the forest. And that each of us was also far away from the war that was going to start up again because the winter was over.

I looked away, I looked at the field and the sky, and Pavel kept on walking by my side.

31

IT WAS MY turn to ride the horse, but I was unlucky. Kyabine was holding the bridle and Sifra was holding my foot. I hoisted myself up but the horse suddenly lurched forward. Kyabine let go of the bridle and I fell to the ground. Then Kyabine ran after the horse. The two of them disappeared. Some time later, Kyabine came back, covered with sweat, without the horse, looking miserable.

We told him that it wasn't his fault, that nobody was strong enough to hold back a horse, and we headed towards the pond.

Around noon, Kyabine and the Evdokim kid went back to the camp to fetch our meals. We played dice while we waited for them. We didn't gamble though. We just tried to make complicated combinations.

Kyabine and the kid returned from the camp with the meals. The kid was carrying our mess tins and our cutlery, Kyabine the big dish that he'd carved from a tree stump over the winter. He was excited when he reached the pond. He asked us if we knew what we were going to eat. We guessed straight away. It was the pig, of course. And there were old potatoes too, and beans. It was a nice stew, and it was still warm because Kyabine and the kid had hurried back. We ate everything and sucked the bones.

Miming compassion, Pavel said: 'There are two lads from the Shuyski regiment who are dreaming of going home so they can eat pork.'

'Poor lads,' I said.

'They'll get to eat chicken,' Kyabine said. 'The woman at the farm had a chicken.'

We stood up and threw the bones in the pond. We were expecting loads of fish to swarm all over them. In fact only two came and swam calmly around the bones.

Pavel and I lay down again. Sifra took off his boots and waded around the edge of the pond. Kyabine washed the big dish, then went into the water and used it to try to catch fish. He slowly lowered it into the water until it was full and then quickly pulled it out, checking to see if there was a fish inside.

The Evdokim kid went to sit on the grass behind us. We heard him take out his notebook. After a while, without turning around, Pavel asked him: 'So tell me, who do you write to if it's not your mother?'

87

It was as if the kid had been expecting this question, because he answered very fast and enthusiastically: 'To myself.'

Pavel raised his eyebrows at me. But what could I say?

Then, still without looking at him, Pavel asked the kid what exactly it was that he was writing.

But it was Kyabine who replied. We thought he was absorbed in his fishing. But he was listening. He said to Pavel: 'Yesterday he wrote that I won at dice.'

'Shut up, Kyabine!' said Pavel.

Kyabine burst out laughing.

Pavel asked again: 'So what is it exactly?'

The kid said: 'Things that I see.'

'Bloody hell,' said Pavel, shaking his head. 'Everything you see in a day!'

Suddenly we couldn't believe our eyes. Kyabine was crouching in front of us, holding the big dish on his knees, and inside it swam a fish so small it could have fitted twice over into the palm of his hand. Kyabine looked at us. He couldn't seem to believe it either. He shouted to Sifra, who was on the other side of the pond: 'Hey, Sifra, come over here, quick!'

'Why?'

'I caught one!'

Sifra came over. He looked at the fish and congratulated Kyabine.

Kyabine wanted to cook and eat his fish, and he wouldn't listen to anyone who tried to dissuade him. Even Sifra joined in: 'There'll be nothing left of it by the time you've cooked it.'

'Why will there be nothing left?' Kyabine asked.

He put the big dish down in front of him, got to his feet, and went to fetch some stones from around the pond. He made several trips, arranged them in a circle, and put a flat stone on top. But the problem was that there was no wood nearby. So he went into the field and returned with his arms full of half-dried grass. He took the fish out of the water, banged its head against the flat stone and laid it on top. He picked up a handful of grass, set fire to it, and slid it between the stones in the circle. It gave off more smoke than flames and quickly burned up. He took another handful and put it inside the circle of stones. He did this at least a dozen times.

The flat stone started to warm up and the fish started to sizzle and smoke. But Kyabine was almost out of grass. He ran into the field and came back with another armful. He stuffed more of it into his little fireplace and blew on the grass. We could smell grilling fish now. He picked it up by the tail and turned it over.

Ever since he'd started doing this, Kyabine had not even glanced up at any of us. All the attention and intelligence he possessed had been focused exclusively on the task of cooking his fish. He had none left for anything else.

We knew this and we were paying attention. We sat there, observing him without moving.

The Evdokim kid had put away his notebook and joined us when he saw the smoke beginning to rise.

Kyabine was lying on his front. His pile of dried grass was close by and he kept digging into it. The pile was getting smaller and smaller. Suddenly there was none left and the fire was out. Kyabine sat up, looked at his fish, grabbed it between his finger and thumb, dropped it in the water in the big dish to cool it down, and ate it in three mouthfuls – head, bones and all – with a thoughtful look on his face. After that, without looking at anyone, he went over to the pond to wash his hands, then came back and lay down next to us.

32

WE STAYED BY the pond all afternoon. We did nothing but talk and sleep, then wake up, lie in the sun and talk again. Strangely, Kyabine didn't try to catch another fish. Occasionally I would see him staring at the surface of the water with a happy, mysterious look on his face. I wondered what his fish tasted like.

When the time came to return to the camp, Pavel suggested we go to Kossarenko's camp to say hello to the lads we'd known in the forest that winter.

Kossarenko's company had built huts in a clearing an hour's walk from ours. Several times, while out searching for firewood, we had bumped into a group of lads doing the same thing. Then, sitting on tree stumps, we'd smoked cigarettes together and discussed how we were heating our huts. After that, we discussed our companies. We tried to work out which company we'd rather be in. We quickly realised that there were pros and cons to each of them, that it was difficult to choose, and that in the end it didn't really matter. Winter would end and we would leave the forest: those were the only things that really mattered, and the only things we could all agree on.

We set off.

We were walking through the field, towards Kossarenko's company. I'd lent my rifle to the Evdokim kid, so he could learn how to carry it in regulation fashion. He was pleased, and I felt lightened.

We heard something moving in the grass and we turned around. All of us stood there in shock. The horse was behind us. We could only see its head and neck above the tall grass. It was covered in white sweat. It looked wild and very beautiful, not at all like the sort of horse that would pull a carriage any more. It lifted up its swollen neck. We could almost hear it breathing. And I'm telling you that it was beauty itself that suddenly appeared and struck us all dumb.

Pavel slowly put his rifle on the ground. He signalled to Kyabine and Sifra to do the same, and he whispered to the Evdokim kid to look after the rifles and wait for us.

At Pavel's signal, we ran towards the horse, spacing out so that we could catch it from behind. We should have left our coats with the kid too. It was difficult to run while we were carrying them. Just as we were about to reach it, the horse suddenly spun and bolted, leaping over the grass.

We sped up.

Sifra and I were on the sides. It was up to us to run as fast as possible, to overtake the horse and then turn to face it.

We moved further and further away from one another.

Sometimes I would catch a glimpse of one of the others.

But in the end I lost sight of them all.

33

I NO LONGER knew where I was.

Nor did I know where the horse was, or any of the others.

I came to a halt. I stood there without moving and listened. I was trying to locate the sound of the pursuit. But my God, that silence! You'd have thought the field was completely deserted.

I waited and I slowly turned my head in the hope that I would pick up the faintest sound of the pursuit from another direction. But still there was just that silence. And it was as if – this is strange, it came to me suddenly – it was as if I was alone in the world once again.

So I spoke in my head to my parents: Don't believe what you see. I told them: There's Pavel, Kyabine and Sifra somewhere in the field, so don't worry.

I sat down in the grass.

I watched the sun sink between the grass stalks, and after a while I lowered my head and began to sob. But, believe me, it wasn't out of sadness.

I said to my parents: You just look at me now, just look. I'm going to get up and I'm going to find the place where the Evdokim kid is looking after our rifles. It's not far from here.

And now I held them both in my arms and I sobbed as I pressed them against me and I swear it wasn't out of sadness.

34

WE CAME BACK to the Evdokim kid, one after another. He was waiting for us, and he handed us our rifles.

We set off again in the dusk.

When we reached the railway tracks, the sun was close to the horizon. It was too late to go and visit Kossarenko's company. The cook wasn't going to wait for us with his ladle. Soon after we'd set off towards the camp, we remembered the stew and we started to run.

We got there in time.

While we were eating the pork stew, the potatoes and the beans, sitting outside the tent, Pavel asked Kyabine: 'What, you're still hungry?'

He was making a joke about the tiny fish that Kyabine had eaten by the pond, of course. Kyabine didn't react.

'Two meals in the same afternoon, eh?' Pavel said. 'You're going to be sick, Kyabine!'

Kyabine stared at him proudly. Then, in a confident voice, he replied: 'No, I won't be sick.'

Night was falling now, and the stew had all been eaten. Our bellies were full. We listened to the sounds of the camp while we sat peacefully on our sleepers. Somewhere there was the sound of metal on metal, though we didn't know what it was. We could hear voices and, where people had lit fires, the sound of wood crackling. From the pine forest came the songs of redwings.

Kyabine rubbed his cheeks with his right hand. He looked happy and inscrutable. His gaze moved to each of us in turn, then he stared at the upturned wooden crate. His hand slid behind his neck and he looked up at the sky. He started to laugh to himself. Then he stopped and watched us again.

After a while, he said: 'You know what?'

We replied that no, we didn't know.

He lowered his head to contain his laughter. When he looked up again, his neck was red and his eyes were bulging.

'What is it, Kyabine?' I asked.

He made a sort of croaking noise.

'Come on, Kyabine, spit it out!' I said.

He took a deep breath and then suddenly boomed: 'There's a pig with fins in my belly!'

I thought we were never going to stop laughing.

35

INSIDE THE TENT we slept on a bed of grass. When we cut the grass, it had been green. Now it had dried. We had to be very careful with the oil lamp because the grass and our blankets could go up in flames. After avoiding a fire in the hut all winter, it would have been really unlucky if it had happened to us now. That was why we always hung the lamp from the pole in the centre, quite high up. The flame was yellow. The draughts of air made it quiver.

When we covered the ground with grass, we hadn't forgotten that it would dry over time and get packed down by the weight of our bodies, so we'd put down a large quantity of grass. It had taken time but we'd been right. Our mattress had packed down but it was still nice and thick.

Pavel and I slept on one side of the pole, and Sifra and Kyabine on the other. The Evdokim kid had found a place near the tent wall, next to Kyabine.

We were warm under our coats and blankets. When we settled down for the night, our breath was white at first because it was still only the beginning of spring. But after a while, thanks to the warmth of our bodies and the flame from the oil lamp, the air in the tent became less cold and our breath grew invisible.

It was Pavel's turn to sleep with the watch. I took it out of my pocket and passed it to him. He placed it on the dried grass, next to his head.

Kyabine had been watching us. 'Kiss her for me, would you?' he asked Pavel.

Pavel picked up the watch and tossed it to him.

'Go ahead, Kyabine.'

Kyabine sat up and found the watch on his blanket. He opened it up and gave it a passionate kiss.

We smiled as we watched him. Then, as he seemed unable to stop, Pavel held out his hand and said: 'All right, that's enough. Give it back now.'

Kyabine closed the watch and handed it over. Pavel put it back in its place by his head.

'What is that?' the Evdokim kid asked Kyabine.

Kyabine didn't know how to answer him. So Pavel answered for him: 'It's a watch.'

'Yeah,' Kyabine said. 'It's a watch.'

The kid must have been thinking that the soldiers of the Red Army kiss their watches before they fall asleep. I didn't like that idea. I asked Pavel to pass it to me for a moment. I opened it and I handed it to the kid so he could see the photograph inside. Then I closed it again and gave it back to Pavel, explaining to the kid that it was just the photograph of the woman that we cared about. That it was nice to sleep with her and that she brought us luck. And with that, I blew out the lamp and covered myself with the blanket.

For a while after that, there was silence. Then, in the darkness, Pavel asked: 'So tell me, lad, what did you see today?'

He was talking to the Evdokim kid, of course. About the things that he wrote in his notebook. The kid took his time before answering, and Pavel was impatient.

'So?'

'I wrote that we ran after some ducks,' the kid said.

'And that we fired at them?' Pavel asked.

'Yes,' the kid said. Cautiously, he added: 'And that you missed them.'

'Well, that's the truth,' Pavel said. Next, he asked: 'Did you say that we stole a horse?'

I heard the dry grass rustling under the kid's shoulders. Embarrassed, he answered: 'Yeah, I said that.'

'That's the truth too,' Pavel said calmly.

The kid must have felt reassured by that, because we

heard him raising himself up on one elbow and then he went on: 'And I said that it escaped before everyone had had a turn riding it, and that that was a shame.'

We all approved this in silence.

Abruptly Kyabine asked: 'Did you say how fast Sifra reassembles his rifle?'

'No, I didn't say that,' the kid replied.

'Shit, you should have done,' Kyabine said, sounding very disappointed. 'Anybody can reassemble a rifle, but nobody can do it as fast as Sifra. And he can do it without even seeing the pieces.'

Then, to Sifra, he said: 'Eh, wouldn't you like him to say it?'

'I don't know,' replied Sifra in his soft voice.

'Oh Sifra!' said Kyabine sadly.

And so, in order not to upset Kyabine, Sifra said: 'All right, yeah, I would like him to say it.'

'Really?'

'Yes, Kyabine.'

'Did you hear that?' Kyabine asked the kid excitedly. 'He'd like it!'

'Yeah.'

'So you won't forget?'

'No, I won't forget.'

Kyabine's satisfaction floated through the tent like steam. Nobody spoke now.

The kid seemed to be waiting for one of us to speak to him again. But, as nothing happened, as nobody said a word, he lay down and stopped moving.

The silence and the darkness covered us.

Then suddenly, almost in a whisper: 'I wrote at the end that we had a good day.'

It was very strange and sweet to hear him say that, because, my God, it was true, wasn't it? It had been a good day. I wished the lamp was still lit so I could see the effect of the kid's words on Pavel, Kyabine and Sifra.

I could tell that nobody was going to say anything else that evening. All of us were probably thinking about what the kid had written in his notebook. Because it had been the last thing we talked about that day, and because none of us knew how to write. Well, I knew a little bit, but I was the only one. And I only knew certain letters – the ones that had been painted in red on the tree trunks when they were delivered to Ovanes' sawmill. They said where the wood had come from. There was a different letter for each district. That's how I came to learn them.

I hadn't used my letters for a long time. But they were still familiar to me. Every time I saw them somewhere, they

102

caught my eye. On crates of ammunition or on the sides of trucks, there was always writing. I didn't know what the words meant, but the letters that I knew leapt out at me as soon as I saw them. And it's funny, but I always wondered what they were doing there. And straight away I would hear, muffled as if it were coming through a wall, the sound of Ovanes' band saw.

36

WE WERE BARELY out of bed before Kyabine started bustling about like a man on a mission. He'd slung Sifra's rifle over his shoulder and he was dusting off his blanket. I stood outside, watching him, wondering what had got into him, and I stamped my feet because it was cold that morning. Around us, steam rose from the other tents and fires were lit to boil water.

Pavel was standing next to me, his coat buttoned up to the collar. 'What the hell are you doing, Kyabine?'

Kyabine did not reply. He'd covered the wooden crate with his blanket and was now smoothing it down with the flat of his hand.

When Sifra returned from pissing behind the tent, Kyabine pointed to one of the sleepers and said: 'Sit down, Sifra.'

'Why?' Sifra asked.

'Oh, please!' Kyabine begged.

Sifra sat on the sleeper and Kyabine told him to wait. Next, he called out to the Evdokim kid, who was still inside the tent. The kid came out and Kyabine gestured for him to sit down on the sleeper facing Sifra. Then he put Sifra's rifle on the blanket that covered the crate and said: 'Go on, Sifra, do it one more time, so the kid can see how you do it again.'

Everybody understood now.

Out of kindness, Sifra did what he was asked. He disassembled his rifle and carefully lined up the pieces on the blanket. Kyabine stood behind him and, as he put his hands over Sifra's eyes, he said to the kid: 'Watch this again, because I don't want you to forget anything. I want you to write exactly how Sifra does it. His skill and all that, you know?'

The kid nodded. Kyabine put his hands over Sifra's eyes. Sifra groped with his hands until he found the first piece, and then it began. Sifra's agile fingers went to work. All the way through, Kyabine watched the kid to make sure he didn't miss anything. When the rifle was reassembled, he dropped his big hands to Sifra's shoulders and stared questioningly at the kid. He wanted to be sure that he had followed Sifra's feat, from beginning to end. The kid nodded and said: 'Got it.'

'You're sure?' Kyabine asked. 'You saw all of it?'

'Yes,' the kid replied.

Kyabine leaned down towards Sifra and said: 'You told me yesterday, that you'd like it.'

'Yes, Kyabine,' Sifra replied.

'When are you going to write it?' Kyabine asked the kid.

'This morning.'

'You'll remember?'

'Definitely.'

'All the details, I mean,' Kyabine said.

The kid touched his index finger to his forehead to indicate that all the details were in there.

37

THEN SUDDENLY THERE were noises coming from all over the camp. People started to move around and talk outside the tents. Our commander appeared in front of the company office. Sergeant Ermakov was with him. We tried to overhear what was being said. Finally the news reached us. We were leaving that night, one hour after Kossarenko's company. We were supposed to follow them from a distance. The order from the general staff had arrived last night. We lowered our eyes as if it was our fault. I just had time to see Kyabine's neck turn red. We kept staring at the ground and withdrew within ourselves, tense and motionless.

'What?' Kyabine asked. 'When do we go?' His head gently bobbed as he spoke and his voice was full of fear.

He'd heard the news, just like we had. But he needed one of us to confirm it for him. I decided to do it myself.

'We're going tonight, Kyabine.'

After that, we each went back to our thoughts. Until

Pavel spoke, we were separated from one another. But then thankfully Pavel said: 'Let's go to the pond now.'

We picked up our rifles and quickly left the camp, trying not to be seen. The last thing we wanted was for Sergeant Ermakov to spot us and order us to dismantle the company office or the kitchen, or to do any of the other things that needed doing before we broke camp.

Nobody spoke on the walk to the pond.

I was walking behind Pavel and my heart was racing. We crossed the field. We no longer cared about crushing the grass. It didn't matter now if we left a path that others could follow. Who would discover the pond and occupy our place once we were gone? Nobody from our company, in any case.

We walked quickly and I could hear the Evdokim kid trotting behind me.

We reached the pond and stood there without moving, staring at the opposite bank. The horse we had stolen yesterday was lying on its side. Its head was halfway into the water. It must have run for a long time after it had escaped from us. It had come here and it had died because nobody had stopped it drinking straight away after running for so long.

We'd seen a lot of dead horses before this, believe me. If we'd laid them side by side, they'd have covered the whole field between the railway tracks and the road. And if we'd had all the dead mules we'd seen, too, there'd have been enough to cover all those horses.

And yet this one made a bigger impression on us than a whole field of dead horses.

We sensed that it had to be done quickly. We walked around the edge of the pond. We each grabbed one of the horse's legs and dragged it with all our strength. We moved it barely a few feet and then paused to catch our breath. The kid had stayed on the far bank and was watching us. I didn't think to ask him to help us. None of us did. Again we bent down and grabbed the horse's legs. Yard by yard, we dragged the horse away from the pond. Until finally it seemed to us that it was far enough away and that the grass would hide it from us when we went back to sit on our bank.

All the same, we stayed there for a while. From where we were, we couldn't see the pond or anything. We got our breath back. At that moment I looked up at the sky above us. But I kept seeing Pavel, Kyabine and Sifra, and the horse between us, and it briefly crossed my mind that nothing existed any more except a dead horse under the sky, and the four of us.

When we returned to our bank, Pavel suddenly started yelling at the Evdokim kid, asking him why he hadn't come to help us. It was unfair but I didn't say anything, and the kid stared despairingly at me. And Pavel asked him, shouting louder and louder, if he knew where all the dead horses were now. If he knew what had happened to them all because nobody had bothered to bury them? They had to be somewhere, all those dead horses we'd seen everywhere all the time.

Pavel was yelling all this despairingly now, frantically rubbing the back of his neck, and the kid continued to look distraught. He didn't even dare to tell Pavel that he didn't know anything about the dead horses.

While this was going on, Sifra stared straight ahead of him so sadly that I thought he might start sobbing at any moment. I don't think I had ever seen Sifra look so sad. And Kyabine sat there with his mouth hanging open, looking even more idiotic than usual, and it was obvious that he was trying to understand what was happening, why Pavel was saying all of this and what his point was. And suddenly the expression on Kyabine's face changed and I understood that he had started thinking about Pavel's question, about the dead horses, that he was trying to come up with an answer so that he could save the kid by replying for him. And then in a trembling voice Kyabine said to Pavel that nobody could know where all the dead horses were, least of all the kid, and the kid looked at Kyabine as if he'd just saved him from drowning.

I thought Pavel was going to get angry with Kyabine, that he was going to yell at him to shut it, that he was going to tell him he was just a big Uzbeki idiot. But he didn't say anything. He didn't shout. In fact, it seemed to calm him down, it seemed to help him. He visibly relaxed. He crossed his hands behind his neck, pressing his forearms against his cheeks, and he stared at the water.

For a moment we all remained motionless like that on the bank.

38

THE SURFACE OF the pond was calm. It was also bright
green, but most of all it was unbelievably calm and I thought
that was lucky because this was surely how I would remember it for ever, given that this was the last time we would
come here. To make sure I would always recall it like this,
so calm and bright, I let my eyes wander over it, slowly
and very attentively. When I came to the place where the
horse's head had been lying in the water earlier, I realised
that I would remember that too and that there was nothing
I could do about it.

My gaze finished its tour of the pond and then I lay on
my back and closed my eyes. The air was still and mild.

All of a sudden I realised that I hadn't yet had time to
remember last night. To recall where I went with Pavel and
whether this time I'd found things to say to him to console
him. I started to think about it.

But as nothing came, I sat up and looked at Pavel. I
thought that would help me remember. I stared at him,

but still nothing came. So I thought that perhaps we simply hadn't gone out last night.

Yes, that was it. It was coming back to me now. He'd touched my arm in the middle of the night, and, just as I'd started getting up so I could go outside with him, he'd tugged on my shoulder to tell me that he'd prefer to stay where we were. I lay back down in bed and I must have fallen asleep again very quickly because I don't remember anything else.

At that moment Pavel asked where the Evdokim kid had gone. We looked around. Then Kyabine called out to him in his booming voice. He appeared almost instantly from behind the grass in the field and came over to sit with us on the bank. He still had a bit of that panic-stricken, despairing look he'd had when Pavel had yelled at him about the horse, and about all the dead horses. He'd unbuttoned his jacket and pulled his sailor's shirt out of his trousers.

'Listen,' said Pavel, not looking at the kid but lying motionless and staring at the surface of the water, 'if there's one thing you ought to write, it's that we're all sad because we have to leave and we won't be able to come back here.'

The kid opened his mouth, but no sound came out.

'Did you hear me?' Pavel asked him. The kid nodded and Pavel went on: 'Yeah, say that we're all sad because we had some good moments here, some really great moments, and we know that we won't have any more, and where we're going there won't be any good moments, because all that is behind us now. You understand? That's what you should write.'

Then he turned to the kid and smiled at him kindly, and in a tight voice he said: 'Yeah, we'd like you to write that.'

Then he fell silent. He looked back at the pond and slowly took his cigarette case out of his pocket. But he didn't open it, he kept it in his hand.

The kid didn't look despairing any more. He stared at Pavel as if he was the brigade commander or even his own father, with an expression of gratitude in his eyes and at the corners of his lips, and it touched me to see that.

Kyabine, Sifra and I said nothing.

What was there to say, after all? Pavel had said it for us. What he'd said was exactly what we all wanted too. We wanted the kid to write about that, about the pond and all that, about all the good moments we'd had here.

There was a long silence then because Pavel wasn't talking any more, he was just lying there motionless with his cigarette case in his hand, and we weren't talking either, so it was completely silent because this morning there wasn't the faintest breath of wind.

39

BUT PAVEL TOLD the Evdokim kid to wait before he started, since he didn't know all the things we'd done at the pond.

We all looked at one another for a moment.

Then we began. We told the kid the things he hadn't seen – everything we'd done at the pond before Sergeant Ermakov brought him to us. We all spoke except for Sifra. He didn't say anything but he looked happy when we mentioned him, especially when I said that it had been his brilliant idea to wash our blankets in the pond.

The kid listened to what we said.

He stared without blinking at whoever was speaking.

At one point I felt sorry for him because we were speaking so fast, and sometimes Kyabine would start talking before Pavel or I had finished what we were saying.

Suddenly we fell silent, because it was over.

The kid took out his notebook and uncoiled the string that held the pencil to it.

As he opened his notebook, he looked at all four of us, sitting in a row on the bank. I nodded to him to signal that it was time for him to get started. 'And try not to forget anything,' I added.

He nodded at me to reassure me that he would.

Pavel started tapping his cigarette case against his knee. Finally he opened it and gave one to each of us. Except to the Evdokim kid, who didn't smoke, and who wasn't paying any attention to us any more anyway because he'd started writing in his notebook. Occasionally he would look up at us briefly before returning to his task.

40

WE SMOKED IN silence. We didn't move much and we were still quite pensive.

We didn't want to move much because the Evdokim kid was writing things that talked about us and our pond. It was really strange and I'm sure the others all felt the same.

Kyabine would sometimes glance at the kid as if he were on the lookout for something. I'm sure that he was thinking about the fish he'd caught and cooked and eaten here, only yesterday, and that he was hoping the kid was going to write that in his notebook since he had witnessed it himself.

He was right to hope for that. I agreed with him that it was one of the good moments we had spent here. The circle of stones that Kyabine had laid to cook the fish was still there, with the blackened flat stone balanced on top of the others. At last I said to the kid, in a low voice so I wouldn't distract him too much: 'Don't forget to talk about Kyabine's fish.'

The kid looked up at me and I gestured at the circle of stones.

'No,' he said, 'I won't forget.'

'Write about him cooking it and all that.'

The kid nodded and went back to his notebook.

Kyabine looked at me and smiled. And then after a while, speaking in a low voice like I had so as not to distract the kid, he called out: 'Pavel!'

'What, Kyabine?'

Kyabine took a breath and whispered: 'So we're leaving tonight, Pavel, huh?'

Of course he'd heard that we were leaving tonight when we were at the camp, and I'd said it to him again just afterwards. But he needed to hear it said another time by one of us. As though, coming from us, it suddenly wasn't such bad news. Pavel understood this. In a considerate voice, he replied: 'Yes, that's right, we're leaving tonight.'

Kyabine stared straight ahead then. He thought for a moment. He picked up a stone from between his legs. He needed to hear us again. In a trembling voice he asked: 'So we're going to continue like we have been, right? We're going to stick together?'

Kyabine knew the answer to this question too. He knew we would continue as we had been. All the same, we signalled to him that obviously nothing would change for the four of us, what did he think, of course we would stick

118

together. Then, in an anxious voice, he said: 'But what if they mix up the companies one day? Pavel, you know they're always doing that.'

There was a silence.

Frightened, Kyabine asked: 'Eh? What would we do?'

'Don't worry, Kyabine,' Pavel told him. 'Even if they mix up the companies, we'll always work things out.'

Kyabine nodded again, and this time he smiled gratefully too. And so, wanting to reassure us in turn – or, actually, no, I think he just wanted to thank us for talking to him like that – but anyway, he said to us: 'Don't worry, I'll always carry the tent.'

Nobody wanted to make fun of him, to say things like 'you'd better' or that they had no intention of helping with that chore.

After that, Kyabine took the stone that he was holding in his hand and threw it in the pond. The surface of the water rippled around the point of impact. A bit further away, a fish jumped out of the water. Kyabine picked up another stone, then he let it drop to the ground between his legs. We were all full of worries and fears, but that morning it was Kyabine – the huge, muscular Uzbeki – who was showing it most.

'It'll be all right, Kyabine,' I told him.

'You really think so?' he asked.

But it wasn't me who answered him. Instead, for once, Sifra spoke without first being asked a question. He just wanted to say something. In his gentle, persuasive voice he told Kyabine: 'Yes, it's true, Kyabine. It'll be all right, because we'll always stick together.'

It did us all good to hear Sifra say that, so gently. It was so unusual to hear any words at all come out of Sifra's mouth that these ones carried special weight. They seemed to bear the stamp of truth. As if the baby Jesus himself had said them. Kyabine appeared to relax.

While this was going on, the Evdokim kid continued to set down in his notebook all those moments we had spent together at the pond, all those moments that were behind us now.

While he was sitting across from us, thinking perhaps about how he was going to write about Kyabine and the fish, I had the strange sensation that if I just stretched out my arm I'd be able to touch the evening with the back of my hand, and that suddenly I'd hear the sound of us raising camp, the tread of our company marching down the road in a column. Walking through the night to who knew where.

But thankfully tonight Kossarenko's company was going to raise camp and set out before us. We were going to follow them at a distance and try to march at the same speed as them so we didn't catch them up.

I thought: Let our company march behind Kossarenko's for as long as possible, sheltered by them, at least until tomorrow morning. And I hoped for Kossarenko's men that there would be no moon tonight and that they would manage to march in complete silence.

41

I FELT THE sun on my back.

I saw it reflected on the surface of the water.

It was good that the water should be calm and the air still today.

Something moved furtively in the grass behind us. Kyabine turned around to look. There was nothing there.

Pavel was sitting next to me. He was breathing slowly. I saw his shoulders rise. He was staring intensely ahead of him.

Then suddenly I started hoping that Kossarenko's company would march before ours for all eternity and that they would eternally hear the first bullets whistle before we did, hear the terrible shells explode, and see before we did everything we feared, may God protect them and forgive me.

42

WHEN THE EVDOKIM kid closed his notebook, he looked satisfied. And because we hadn't wanted to move while he was writing, because we'd just stayed where we were, sitting motionless in a row under the burning sun, we were beginning to feel hot in our coats.

It wouldn't have made much difference to the kid if we'd moved while he was writing. He didn't need us any more, because he knew exactly what he had to say. But since he would sometimes glance up and observe us briefly, we had the impression that it might help him if we were always in sight, so we didn't stir.

We waited until he'd put his notebook away in his jacket pocket.

Only then did we take off our coats.

Pavel spread his out on the grass behind us. He walked over to the water and said: 'Let's stay here.'

He turned around and looked at us. He calmly sized us up and said: 'Let's stay here, eh? What do you think?'

I nodded. 'Yeah, let's stay. Ermakov can go fuck himself. There are plenty of other idiots to help him dismantle the company office.'

Coldly smiling, Pavel added: 'There are plenty of other poor idiots who can march tonight too. But not us. We're going to stay here.'

I quickly went over what he had just said. I heard it as clearly as an echo, and I said: 'What do you mean, Pavel? Why are you talking about tonight?'

He didn't answer. The sun was in his eyes, so he pushed down the visor of his cap. It made a line of shadow over his eyes, though I could still see them sparkling from the darkness.

Next to me, Kyabine had started to fidget when Pavel pushed down his visor. Pavel's words were slowly starting to percolate in his head.

Pavel addressed him: 'We're fine here, aren't we, Kyabine?'

Kyabine lowered his head, then looked up and answered in an anxious voice: 'Yes, we're fine.'

Pavel spread out his arms and lifted his hands up to Kyabine, as if to point to both him and his answer. Then he turned back to the pond and lifted up the visor on his cap. Suddenly, his back to us, he said: 'So why should we start marching again like dead men?'

124

Kyabine, Sifra and I were all alone with that now. All three of us were helpless and anxious because we had understood what it was Pavel was suggesting. And now he had turned his back on us and seemed to want to stay silent.

So in a weak voice I called out to him: 'Pavel!'

'What?'

In a whisper I said: 'What are you talking about, Pavel? Why wouldn't we go back to camp tonight?'

Instead of replying to me, Pavel – still with his back to us, facing the pond – said to Kyabine: 'Hey, Kyabine, wouldn't you like to catch some more fish?'

Kyabine looked at Sifra and me in a panic. His idiot's eyes blinked and rolled.

Patiently, Pavel said: 'Go ahead, Kyabine, answer me!'

Kyabine answered honestly: 'Yes, I'd like to.' Then he added: 'But they're too small, really, aren't they?'

Pavel nodded, then said: 'But what if there are some bigger ones, Kyabine?'

'I haven't seen any,' Kyabine replied. 'All I've seen are little ones.'

Still facing the pond, Pavel explained: 'Yeah, but you can always throw the little ones back in the water until you catch a big one. I'm sure there are some big ones swimming at the bottom of the pond. I bet if all four of us tried, we could catch some. You can cook them, Kyabine – you've got the knack. And afterwards we'll eat them. And tonight we'll sleep here, and if it rains we'll go to the station to sleep. We can clean the station up and take a load of grass there to sleep on. From time to time, we'll requisition blankets and tobacco, and at night we'll go back to the station. And we can bring back a chicken and some leeks when we've had enough of eating fish.'

'Maybe we could try to catch the big ones tonight?' Kyabine asked excitedly.

'Yeah, why not,' said Pavel kindly.

On a roll, Kyabine added: 'We can cook them on my stones and afterwards we can go back to the company.'

Pavel did not move or speak.

'Eh, Pavel, what do you think?' Kyabine said. 'Can we try to catch some now?'

In a sad voice, Pavel said: 'Yeah, if you want to, Kyabine.'

Then Kyabine, his throat tight, asked desperately: 'But afterwards we'll go back to the company, right?'

A long silence followed, as empty as a day's march.

Then Pavel nodded.

In a sudden panic, Kyabine said: 'But we don't have the big mess dish. We didn't bring it with us!'

'What?'

'We need the big dish to catch the fish,' Kyabine explained. 'How else can we do it?'

At that, he set off abruptly, without a second thought, towards the camp. I told him to come back. 'What the hell are you doing?' I said. 'If Ermakov sees you, he'll make you stay at the camp all day to help him dismantle the company office.'

But, leaping through the tall grass, he yelled back over his shoulder: 'I'm clever. He won't see me.'

He disappeared into the grass.

I tried again to make him come back. But in the distance we heard: 'I'm clever!'

But the truth was, he wasn't. Not Kyabine. He was stronger than Pavel, Sifra and me put together. He was incredibly strong and loyal, and he had a voice like thunder. But clever? No.

For an instant I thought about running after him, but I had no chance of catching him now.

Pavel crouched in front of the pond. He pushed the visor of his cap back up his forehead. He plunged his hands into the still water. He let them float on the surface for a moment. Then he took them out again and wet his face. Time had passed and the sun had risen higher in the sky.

43

SIFRA SAT DOWN and balanced his rifle on his knees.

He had listened to all of that in silence, sometimes shooting us frightened, helpless looks, as if we were his mother and father and we were deciding his future.

That was all he'd done.

But I don't want you to think that Sifra just skulked near us like a shadow. No, that's not how he was. I want you to know that, on the contrary, he was always with us, gentle and attentive, with that gentle, prophetic look in his eyes, and almost always silent. I would really like you to understand him.

44

KYABINE SUDDENLY APPEARED from the grass behind us, carrying the big mess dish over his head. 'Told you I was clever, didn't I?' he shouted.

And it was true: he had been clever. He must also have been very lucky. He took off his boots and went into the water. We asked him what was happening in the camp, if the others had started taking their tents down yet. 'I didn't look,' he answered as he waded into the water.

'What do you mean, you didn't look?' asked Pavel, stunned.

'No, I didn't look.'

When he was in the pond up to his knees, Kyabine turned around and asked the Evdokim kid: 'If I catch a big one, you'll add that, won't you?'

The kid said yes, of course he would add it. Kyabine bent down and plunged the big dish into the water, and after that he stopped moving. Soon afterwards he yelled that he'd got one. He came back to the bank and we all crowded round to see the fish. It wasn't big. Kyabine sat down and put the dish between his legs. We asked him if he was going to eat it. He said no, he just wanted to watch it swim. We left him to watch his fish.

I was standing on the bank, trying not to think about anything, or at least not about tonight, when Kyabine called out to me: 'Benia, come and see.'

His voice was mysterious.

He signalled for me to sit down next to him and in silence he showed me something that was floating in the air. It was a tiny bit of grass. It stayed there on its own, hovering in the air like that, just in front of our eyes, and it was really surprising. Then I spotted a sort of spider's thread. It was almost invisible, and the bit of grass was suspended from the end of it. Kyabine didn't see the thread.

While I was wondering if I should point it out to him, we heard gunshots from the camp. Three shots, with spaces in between. We understood. When the last one had faded to silence, Kyabine stood up, evading the bit of grass which was still floating there in the air, and he went to throw his fish back in the water. We picked up our coats and our rifles and we looked at Pavel, thinking that perhaps he was going to say something about the pond. But he didn't say anything, and we left.

45

WE WERE SITTING on our railway sleepers. Our bags were packed, our blankets rolled up and tied underneath them. We'd folded up the tent and it was ready to be fastened to Kyabine's back. All over the camp, they were waiting, just like us, each man sitting next to his belongings. Evening fell. This was the first time since we'd come out of the forest that not a single fire crackled and glowed here at dusk. We could hear almost nothing. Occasionally the lads next to us whispered things to each other.

The Evdokim kid had gone to talk with the other kids, the ones who'd walked up the railway tracks with him.

Sifra was next to me. I said to him that at least we were leaving with clean blankets. He said we should have washed our coats too. I said yeah, it was a shame that we hadn't done that. And suddenly I wished we had one more day here, so we could go to the pond to wash our coats, and frantically rub away the dirt to celebrate that extra day. And why not have another extra day to let them dry in the sun?

Kossarenko's company entered our camp. Kossarenko was marching at the front with a sergeant. Just behind them, a man led five mules. They were good, fat mules. They must have requisitioned those mules, because their own mules – the company's mules, I mean – had been eaten in the forest, like ours.

The company halted. Our commander went over to Kossarenko. They shook hands. Our commander took out a cigarette case and they started talking.

It was too dark now to recognise the men from Kossarenko's company who we'd met in the forest last winter.

When Kossarenko and our commander had finished their cigarettes, Kossarenko talked to the mule-driver and his sergeant. Some of the lads from their company took the bags off two of their mules and divided them between the three others. Our commander called out to someone from our company to take the two mules. Then he looked at his watch. Just after that, Kossarenko gave the order to leave, and while his company was getting ready, I thought to myself: In an hour, that will be us.

When the company disappeared into the night, Pavel, who had been sitting on the sleeper across from me until then, stood up. He looked all around and he seemed to be listening for something.

'What are you doing, Pavel?' I asked.

He didn't reply. He just shook his head and sat back down on the sleeper. Suddenly Kyabine asked me: 'So how does it stay there on its own like that?'

'What?'

And then I remembered. He was talking about the bit of grass that was floating in the air.

'I don't know, Kyabine,' I lied. 'It just does.'

He was disappointed by this response. But I thought I'd done the right thing. All of a sudden I wanted to tell Kyabine not to worry and I wanted this hour to be over and us to be marching because all four of us were sad and lost and we were so afraid. And if I'd known, I'd have taken all three of them in my arms and then they'd have been so embarrassed, and God, so would I, but having said it, having suddenly thought it, I have the impression that I actually did it and now I'm even sadder.

The hour passed and we left.

46

WE MOVED THROUGH the darkness, between fields.

I walked next to Pavel. In front of us were Kyabine and the Evdokim kid. And in front of them was Sifra. Kyabine was carrying the tent on his back and his bag on his chest. The Evdokim kid was carrying the tent pole and his blanket.

We didn't know how far the company was stretched out on the road because it was too dark to see.

The sky was dark too – it looked like the plain upside down – and sometimes the moon illuminated the edges of clouds and the fields, and all the men in the company that we could see had strange silhouettes then because of the way they were carrying their loads, because of the blankets, bags and guns and all the other junk that they had on their backs.

Some of them had their tin cup and plate tied to their belts next to each other and they kept clanking together, making a continual racket. Those men were real idiots.

But I guessed that the company must be stretched out quite a long way because the mules that Kossarenko had given us – the mules that were walking at the front of the column – well, we hadn't heard their horseshoes for quite some time.

All we heard was the metal clanking of the idiots.

Someone said: 'Hey, put your pans away!'

Someone replied: 'Shut your mouth!'

Sergeant Ermakov wasn't far away. Somewhere ahead of us, he shouted into the night: 'I'll shut you all up in a minute! Silence!'

Then one of those idiots started singing in a low voice. He sang so softly that we couldn't understand the words. But we quickly realised that he was singing in time with the clanking of his tin cup against his plate.

Kyabine turned back to Pavel and me, and he nodded in the direction of where the song was coming from. He seemed to like it.

The man who was singing did not keep it up very long. Either he ran out of breath or he just didn't feel like it any more. We continued advancing through the darkness, and sometimes someone would cough or whisper something, and strangely, at the moment when they fell silent again, we became aware that it was nighttime. And I thought: At least tonight Pavel won't wake up in terror because he's dreaming that Sifra has cut his throat. I was happy for him, and for

Sifra too. Or at least I tried to think I was. Because in reality I wasn't completely happy. It had always been thanks to Pavel's nightmares that I'd been able to spend those moments alone with him. And so I felt a bit ashamed that I couldn't feel completely happy for Pavel and Sifra.

We heard a rumbling noise ahead of us. It grew closer, then it passed us on the bridge. Because of the noise and the darkness, we weren't able to tell if there was any water under the bridge.

The rumbling of the wooden planks faded behind us. Then we didn't hear anything any more.

We marched in silence. Nobody spoke.

The strangest, funniest silhouette of all those in front of us was Kyabine's, loaded as he was with the tent and his bag, and with the butt of his rifle appearing to come out of his neck.

I asked Pavel in a whisper how he was. He replied that he was fine. Kyabine turned around because he heard us. I asked him the same question. He told me everything was all right. And at that, he touched Sifra's shoulder. Sifra turned around and signalled that he was fine. The Evdokim kid seemed to be holding up too. Sometimes he would lift his head and look up at the sky.

47

WE STOPPED FOR a rest. We didn't know how long we'd been walking. We were out of breath. Pavel, Kyabine, Sifra, the kid and I sat on our bags in the middle of the road and we spread our blankets over our backs before the cold of the night could freeze us.

Sergeant Ermakov ordered everyone to their feet. The ones who'd lain down in the field to sleep for a while were herded onto the road. Some of them had actually fallen asleep and they made strange movements when they got up, blinking confusedly in the darkness as they tried to work out where they were.

The kid had taken off his felt peasant boots and was holding his ankles. Pavel was staring at something over my shoulder.

We caught our breath. Slowly the air moved under our blankets and froze our sweat.

Suddenly Kyabine said to the kid: 'We had a really nice hut in the forest.'

The kid looked at him.

'With a stove,' Kyabine added. 'Eh, Pavel? Didn't we?'

'Yeah, we did,' said Pavel.

'But Pavel,' Kyabine asked, 'why did we burn them?'

Pavel shrugged. But this wasn't enough for Kyabine, so he asked me: 'Eh? Why did we burn the huts?'

'Because we didn't need them any more, Kyabine.'

'You think?'

'Of course.'

And then, as he often did when something was troubling him, Kyabine lost interest in us and started thinking.

The kid was still holding his ankles when the order came to start marching again. I stayed next to him because he was struggling to get his boots back on. He seemed terrified of being left behind and he started getting more and more anxious. 'Don't worry,' I told him, 'I'll wait for you.'

That was when he realised that he'd been putting them on the wrong feet. All the others had left when he stood up and started rolling up his blanket.

'I'd keep it on for a while longer if I were you,' I advised him.

He put it back over his shoulders. He picked up the tent pole and we set off.

He was very grateful that I'd waited for him and he held

the pole very straight. We were the last ones in the column. Pavel, Kyabine and Sifra were too far ahead for us to see them.

'How do you feel?' I asked him.

'Fine.'

'Good.'

'Are we going to march all night?' he asked me.

'I guess so.'

We said all this in a whisper, because of the darkness.

'Did you manage to write everything about the pond?' I asked.

'Nearly everything, yeah.'

'Take your time.'

'Yeah. But I've nearly finished.'

To take his mind off things, I said: 'Don't forget Kyabine's fish.'

'I won't.'

'You've seen how much it matters to him.'

'Yeah.'

'So, listen,' I said, carefully choosing my words. 'When you've finished with the pond, there's something else I'd like you to write.' I paused, to plan even more carefully what I had to say. 'Listen, what I'd like you to write about . . . well, it's Pavel. I'd like you to write that Pavel and me . . . that we

139

were really lucky to find each other. It was lucky too for Kyabine and Sifra, of course, but with Pavel . . . well, shit, you understand, don't you? It was even luckier, you know?'

'Yeah, I understand.'

He listened very attentively.

'Write it how you want, and take your time.'

He nodded.

I waited for a moment and then I said: 'Has Pavel said anything to you that's a bit like what I said about him?'

'No.'

I started walking faster.

'Come on, let's catch up with the others.'

We marched and marched and we caught up with them and we continued marching and marching through the night, and sometimes we would pass through a village or a dark forest. And for a long time nobody in the company spoke – not us nor anybody around us.

I was walking with Sifra at one point, and then with Pavel, and then I lost sight of them and suddenly I realised that I was walking on my own, next to someone in the company whose name I didn't know.

48

SOMETIMES WE WOULD march past Sergeant Ermakov as he stood by the side of the road, leaning on his rifle. And long before we reached him, we could hear him telling us to advance.

What did he think we were doing?

The company left the road and entered a field. Far in the distance on the left there was a dark line: it was the edge of a forest and now we could see stars shining above it, between black clouds.

We walked through the short grass. Around me and in front of me, I caught sight of bowed, staggering figures. And they stretched out as far ahead of me as I could see.

I was still walking on my own. I tried to spot Kyabine's enormous silhouette, but he must have been out of sight in the darkness, or somewhere behind me. My fingers tightened suddenly and I thought I'd lost my rifle. In fact I'd fastened it across my bag, but I didn't remember that at the time.

I thought I could see Pavel up ahead. I didn't have enough strength to catch him up. I called out to him. But nobody replied or turned around.

I thought to myself: Either it's not him or he didn't hear me.

Soon after this, the order came through that we were stopping. Most of the men lay down where they were as soon as they heard it, but I kept walking, steering my way between them as I went in search of the others. I found Sifra first, then I heard Kyabine calling out to us. We headed towards him. Pavel came too, accompanied by the Evdokim kid.

We sat in the grass without even thinking about unstrapping our bags. We were all hollow-eyed, our mouths agape. The kid rolled onto his side with a groan. Pavel leaned down and said: 'Don't fall asleep now.'

The kid didn't move and he didn't reply.

'Did you hear me? You mustn't fall asleep. Have a rest but don't fall asleep.'

He spoke to him gently. The kid nodded. I helped him to sit up. He was wild-eyed and there was white spittle at the corners of his mouth. I took off my bag and wedged it under his back. A moment later, he lowered his head and started to sob.

'It's all right, lad,' I told him. 'We're all here.'

Kyabine kept staring at the kid. It made him sad and shy to see the kid sobbing like that.

Suddenly, realising that I couldn't remember, I asked who had the watch tonight.

Pavel took it out of his pocket. I held out my hand and he passed it to me. I opened it and kissed the photograph. Kyabine kissed it passionately, and even Sifra gave it a shy peck because Kyabine asked him to, and it was touching to see him do it because he never had before. I was happy that he'd done it at last, and even though we knew that the watch didn't really bring us luck, I thought to myself: Well, why shouldn't it bring us luck? Pavel took it back and then handed it to the Evdokim kid.

'Go on, you too.'

He almost stopped sobbing. He held the watch in his hand and looked at us.

'Open it and kiss the picture,' I said, to encourage him.

He did it and then he handed the watch back to Pavel. We spread our blankets over our backs and the sky started to turn blue far off to our left, above the forest. Pavel took out his cigarettes and gave one to each of us. They tasted really awful and bitter, but we smoked them down to the filter and afterwards we concentrated on fighting off sleep. It was hard for the kid.

When dawn broke, we were still there, sitting in the field, and we could see where we were now, and where all the others in the company were, all around us, and lots of them were asleep. The mules that Kossarenko had given us were standing next to each other, eating grass, with all the boxes from the company office and all the cook's things still loaded on their backs.

Sergeant Ermakov's voice echoed over the field: 'No fires!'

Other voices passed on this message:

'No fires!'

'No fires!'

And then someone else called out in the same peremptory tones: 'No women!'

For once, Ermakov didn't lose his temper because someone had made a joke. In fact, he even replied with one of his own: 'Women are allowed, but only if they're pretty.'

'And I bet you've got loads of pretty women in your pocket, haven't you, sarge?'

'Yeah, come over here and I'll give you one.'

'Coming!'

In the distance were some tiny narrow sheds painted in all different colours, and there was the big forest to the left that ended at the foot of a low hill, and behind the hill there was a town. We couldn't see the town but we could see threads of grey smoke rising up and forming a flat cloud that drifted over the forest.

There was a town somewhere behind the hill, and it was wonderful news that we would soon see a town again. Kaliakine, our commander, stood to the side on his own. He had a blanket over his shoulders too and he was staring in the direction of the sheds.

49

WHEN IT CAME time to get up again, we had to wake the men who'd fallen asleep and they were shaky and dazed as they struggled to their feet, and in their eyes you could see dreadful glimmers. You had the impression that they were ready to kill the ones who'd woken them.

We reformed our ranks and set off towards the colourful sheds. They were built at the ends of patches of garden that the owners had started to plough, and in places you could see the tops of vegetables emerging from the earth. Sergeant Ermakov told us to be careful not to tread on them. Although it was really too late, because it looked like Kossarenko's company had passed this way before us: the gardens were already badly damaged.

All the same, we tried to be careful and the ranks came apart. The whole company became scattered.

Pavel and I went into a yellow-painted shed. There was no window and it was dark inside. At the back of the shed, we found some rope and a nicely sharpened pickaxe.

Kyabine, Sifra and the Evdokim kid were waiting for us outside. Brandishing the pickaxe, Pavel said we'd be able to dig trenches around the tent to protect us from the rain. He broke the handle in half to make it less cumbersome to carry. We heard the first gunshots and the shells exploded at the front of the column with a terrible roar. The mules bolted at a gallop towards the edge of the forest while huge clods of earth flew from where the shells had hit.

All over the gardens, men were screaming. We threw ourselves to the ground. I fell on top of Kyabine and rolled onto my back. The kid was kneeling behind one of the sheds. He held the tent pole in both hands, as if he were clinging to it. Pavel ordered him to lie down. Sifra crawled up behind us. When he reached us, a second salvo came from the edge of the forest, and this time the shells exploded closer to us. A shed was blown into the air. Bits of plank fell back down to earth. We covered our heads with our bags. Yassov, the hand sculptor, crawled past us. He was moving fast, heading for one of the sheds. We heard men calling out behind us. Further ahead, one started screaming that he'd been hit. We waited but they didn't fire again and soon – apart from the man who was screaming – silence descended over the gardens again. I lifted my head to look over at the forest. Nothing moved. I didn't see anything. The mules had vanished. All I saw was the dark line of undergrowth. I told the others that I didn't see anything.

Pavel lifted his head too. I heard Sifra loading his rifle. Then Kyabine started crawling over to the Evdokim kid. Pavel asked him what he was doing. Kyabine replied that he was going to see the kid. The man who'd been screaming fell silent. And now we didn't hear anything at all.

They had heavy artillery over there, and probably machine guns too. They were waiting for us to get up and start running in the open. But where were we supposed to run to? We didn't know. Kyabine was now close to the kid, who was lying behind the shed. He'd covered the kid's head with the tent. Sifra was aiming his rifle at the forest. We heard murmurs as the men started to talk and call out to one another. And the man who'd stopped screaming now let out a piercing howl. Sifra touched my shoulder and pointed to the mules, which were running past the forest towards the hills. I rolled onto my back and tried to see where we would start running when the time came. The only safe place was behind us, opposite the forest, where the gardens ended. I could see a road and behind it a vast field that sloped up a long way towards a plateau.

The order came through to pull out. After that there was a silence, finally broken by Commander Kaliakine's whistle.

The whole company stood up and started running away from the forest. Kyabine and the Evdokim kid came over to us and we all ran together. Kyabine was carrying the tent under one arm. We heard the rattle of their machine guns and, almost immediately afterwards, the boom of their artillery shells.

The ones who were hit started yelling at us to wait for them. Sergeant Ermakov yelled even louder that we must not stop. So we ran. The bullets whistled, and when a shell landed, its explosion was all that we heard. We reached the road and dived into the ditch that ran alongside it: first Pavel, the kid and me, then Kyabine and Sifra. We rolled to the botton of the ditch and caught our breath. Suddenly Kyabine sat up and started calling Sifra's name at the top of his voice, as if he were still back at the other end of the gardens. But he was with us in the ditch. He was covered in blood. He seemed to be looking at us all and, at the same time, staring into space. Pavel lifted up Sifra's head and Sifra let out a scream that no words could ever describe. Pavel carefully lowered his head back and signalled to him that he wouldn't touch him again.

Sifra appeared to be staring at the sky now, his jaw trembling, and the despair in his eyes . . . never had I seen anything like it. I'd never seen anything like the despair in

Kyabine's eyes either. The rest of our company had jumped over the ditch and crossed the road and now they were running up the field towards the safety of the plateau. A deep silence fell, because the firing had ceased. But I could see them coming out of the forest, moving towards us with their machine guns on tripods. And Kyabine knelt close to Sifra and he couldn't bring himself to look at him but kept looking from Pavel to me and back again, and suddenly Pavel told him to take the kid and run with him to the plateau. Kyabine kissed Sifra's leg, as far away as possible from his wound, then he grabbed the tent, took the kid by one arm, and they climbed out of the ditch and crossed the road. Pavel told Sifra to close his eyes. Sifra did as he was told and Pavel's hand stroked his cheek, then he stood up, aimed the barrel of his rifle at the back of Sifra's neck, and fired. Then we climbed out of the ditch, ran across the road and started up the slope of the field. We passed Commander Kaliakine, who stood with his revolver in his hand. The machine guns started to rattle again. When we caught up with Kyabine and the Evdokim kid, our throats were burning and the bullets whistled everywhere through the air and landed in the earth.

The men in our company who had already reached the crest of the plateau were lying behind it and firing at the machine guns in the distance with their rifles, screaming insults because our rifles didn't carry far enough.

Soon we reached the crest. The kid, who was running in front of me, let go of the tent pole and fell to the ground. He'd been hit by several bullets. I ran past him and picked up the tent pole without stopping, and suddenly I dropped to the ground and turned around and began crawling back to the kid. I opened up his jacket and took his notebook.

50

BEFORE THEY REACHED the road below us and came within range of our rifles, we retreated from the crest, fleeing towards the hills, and each hill looked just like the last one, covered in the same forest, as if we were constantly retracing our steps, eternally following the same paths that wound around the hills as if there was nowhere to go.

Around noon, Sergeant Ermakov did a head count.

We were under some trees and while he counted us, nobody looked at him. Kaliakine, our commander, stood apart, stooped and pensive, his blanket over his shoulders and his whistle swinging as it hung from his neck.

In the evening we pitched our tents on the side of a hill. Pavel used the pickaxe to dig a flat spot in the slope. We lit our lamp and hung it from the pole and on the canvas we could see our shadows and the shadow of the smoke from the oil lamp. Kyabine was lying on his side. Pavel was lying on his back, eyes wide open. I was sitting between them and looking outside through the gap in the tent. But the flame of the lamp was so close to my eyes that I couldn't see anything outside. Kyabine suddenly burst into sobs. The sobs seemed to come through his nose and they made the strangest and most horrible sound.

After a while, Pavel said: 'Stop, Kyabine!'

Kyabine didn't stop. Pavel waited a bit longer, grinding his teeth, then barked: 'Stop it!'

But Kyabine continued making that horrible, heart-rending sound.

Pavel leaned on an elbow: 'Shut your bloody mouth!'

Kyabine got to his feet and rushed at Pavel, knocking me over on the way. He pinned Pavel down between his legs, clasped his huge hands over Pavel's throat, and started screaming things – strange, incomprehensible, heart-rending things – while Pavel closed his eyes, making no attempt to struggle against the hands that were strangling him.

Then Kyabine let him go. He went back to his corner of the tent, lay down on his side in the same spot, and he didn't move or make a sound. Pavel got his breath back. The lamp was swinging crazily and the shadows that spun around the tent looked unreal.

Finally the lamp stopped swinging and I remembered the notebook. I took it from my pocket and put it on my knees. It fell off, so I picked it up and opened it.

I shouldn't have done that. The Evdokim kid didn't know how to write any better than I did, with my five letters. A few pages were covered with these letters, all lined up neatly, but none of them, I could tell, formed a word.

I picked up the pencil. I ached with the desperate desire to draw a letter. But at that moment I didn't dare. I put the pencil back in the notebook, and the notebook in my pocket, and I went out of the tent.

I could see the shapes of other tents. I could hear moans and ahead of me the sky was black.

All the Evdokim kid knew how to write were some poor little letters lined up in a row. And so I started to think furiously about what would become of the pond and the dead horses, of Sifra's skill and all those who die and who are our brothers.

I stood outside the tent, on the hillside, facing the sky. The notebook dug into my stomach and again I ached to write in it, but already I guessed, already I had the intuition, even before having begun, that the sky is endless and that there aren't the words.

And I think to myself now that all those years have passed: Where is he today, Sifra? Who looked after him? So many years have passed and I wonder where Sifra is and who looked after him, where is the dust of his bones and how